REVOLUTIONARY SPARK

THE MOLLY WESTON CHRONICLES

Books in the Molly Weston series:
Revolutionary Heart
Revolutionary Spirit

Other books by the author:
Caesar and Cleo Find the Purrrrfect Christmas Tree
Riglee Celebrates Thanksgiving
Riglee Rolls an Easter Egg

Revolutionary Spark
The Molly Weston Chronicles

Lori Piotrowski

Dedication

For patriots, young and old, who love the United States.
May long this nation prosper as a beacon of freedom.

Revolutionary women…shared with cheerfulness and gaiety the
privations and sufferings to which the situation of their country
exposed them. In every stage of this severe trial, they displayed
virtues that have not always been attributed to their sex.
With a ready acquiescence, with a firmness always cheerful,
and a constancy that never lamented all the sacrifices…they
yielded up the conveniences furnished by wealth and commerce,
consenting to share the produce of their labour. They even
gave up without regret a considerable portion of the covering
designed for their own families, to supply the wants of a distressed
soldiery; and heroically suppressed the involuntary sigh which the
departure of their brothers, sons and husbands for camp,
rendered from their bosoms.

—Chief Justice John Marshall, 1804

My eyes never beheld such a funeral. The procession extended
further than can be imagined. This shows there are many more
lives to spend, if wanted, in the service of their country.
It shows…that the ardour of the people is not to be quelled
by the slaughter of one child.

—John Adams on the funeral of Christopher Snider, February 1770

TABLE OF CONTENTS

A Note to the Reader

When embarking on writing historical fiction, writers quickly find they will cross a fine line. What is true? Can we trust the sources? This fine line became somewhat gritty as I learned of Christopher Snider's death while reading issues of the *Boston Gazette*. This child, often referred to as Christopher Seider in other documents, was someone I felt deserved more tribute than history has given him. As I dug into my research, I became convinced that Christopher's death was a significant factor in the American colonies' decision to sever their ties with Great Britain. According to the *Gazette* and other sources, more than two thousand townspeople turned out for the funeral cortege, about 13 percent of the city! So much of history focuses on the Boston Massacre—a divisive event in its own right—but I believe it might not have happened, or the consequences might not have been so severe, had young Christopher not been killed. I leave it up to the readers to make their own determination.

February 1768

Molly Weston

"That can't possibly be true!"

"What are you referring to, Molly?"

Mother and I rolled dough into biscuits, well, mostly she rolled as I'd dusted off my hands to read the Monday advices in the *Gazette.*

"Some man, who probably has never tried this, wants us to follow a new receipt to replace tea.

> Small common Field Peas, burnt carefully with Butter, and ground as Coffee, has been tryed by several Persons in this Town, and found equal, if not superior, to the Produce of the West Indies. —Quere, How many Thousands may be saved annually by this Discovery?[1]

"Well, it might make a tasty warm drink, but to substitute peas for tea leaves? Ha! I scoff at the very idea!"

"Daughter, whatever makes sense to avoid buying tea is worth trying. We may even save a few pennies! Let's experiment. Do we have any dried peas left from our summer harvest? Perhaps we could plump them with water and try this receipt."

"I'd rather drink that Labrador concoction!"

Mother clucked and smiled, knowing full well I'd never touch that brew—my mouth puckered at the memory! Merchants have been gathering herbs from the lake country to quench the Bostonians' thirst for tea, but rumors flew of people falling ill from drinking the beverage. We believed that Tory merchants selling tea imports on the side were spreading the rumors.

"Elizabeth! Are you here?"

Mother and I looked up to see a friend, Sally Bartholomew, turn the corner from the great room into the kitchen. Her deep blue mantua, trimmed in luxurious beaver, billowed behind her. Her eyes swept the kitchen and landed on the table dusted with flour and mounded with biscuit dough.

"Oh, I see you're busy."

"What brings you over, Sally?" Mother asked.

"We hadn't seen you for a while, and I thought you'd want to know that Alice isn't feeling well. Abigail and I plan to go and see her this afternoon. Won't you join us?"

Mother gave me a knowing look. She still had friends who'd hoarded their own supply of tea for "medicinal" purposes, and even some of the girls in my age group "visited" their ill friends every afternoon—all a subterfuge to partake of the prohibited beverage. In some weeks, a different friend fell ill every day, allowing women to tend to their "ailing" friends on a rotating schedule.

"I'm sorry to hear about Alice," she replied, "but Molly and I have quite a few chores this afternoon."

"Surely you could spare an hour, Elizabeth. It's been so long since we've seen you."

Sally's reaction showed the true reason she dropped in to see us.

"It's not that we're always so busy," I added, "but Mother and I believe in upholding the boycott. We're not taking tea."

"Don't speak nonsense! It's not part of the boycott if you already had the tea." Sally's tone took on a supercilious note.

Rather than ship tea, fabric, and other goods back to their country of origin when the boycott began, merchants loaded the cargo into their warehouses. For safekeeping, they said, until the boycott ends. Tea exchanged hands in dark warehouses, yet partisan proprietors openly brewed and served the drink in their coffee houses. Mother and I abstained and encouraged our friends to do likewise, although our efforts met with resistance. The tea trade continued to flourish within the city.

I sighed loudly and cut dough into square biscuits.

"Sally, thank you for coming over, but our decision is firm. We don't want to give anyone more reason to speak ill of our efforts." With that, Mother rose to escort her friend to the door.

Peter Oliver, brother to Stamp Master Andrew Oliver and close friend of Lt. Governor Thomas Hutchison, ridiculed our boycott, writing regularly in the newspapers about the women's social gatherings.

Oliver isn't wrong when he talks about the women's visits as a ruse to drink tea, but I hated the idea that this loyalist could be right about anything. It was good to know that Mother supported me.

Mother and I chatted as we finished cutting biscuits and put them in the oven. Soon, the aroma of baking bread quickly dispelled the sour atmosphere Sally's visit had brought. The hearth warmed the room, melting the tiny snowbanks on the windowsills as well as the chill in our hearts.

We had another reason to be cheerful as well. Finally, Eli and Paul were back home. Their arrest last November had shaken our family.

♥

Worried about retribution from their participation in the Stamp Act riots and subsequent destruction of General Bridgewater's cache of black powder, my brothers had moved out of the tavern and lived by felling timber in the nearby forests where the government claimed the trees as property of the Crown. The Royal Navy needed to build up its supply of warships to counter the threat posed by the ever-growing Spanish fleet. As timber grew scarce in England, the Crown searched for another source. They found it in America, where the tallest and straightest white pine grew plentiful, and the best of these trees were marked to become masts and spars in the Royal fleet.

Before long, the two, along with Eli's best friend Cotton and a few other men, began to stash some of the choicest logs. Never too many at once, but enough so that the Crown couldn't lay claim to all the forest. This attempt to foil the British from pillaging a valuable resource succeeded for several months, until a platoon of British regulars intercepted a missive and raided the logging camp. Although Cotton escaped capture, others, including Eli and Paul, were imprisoned.

Father turned to Samuel Adams for assistance, who, in turn, asked his relative John Adams to step in. With a lawyer of his stature, we felt sure that the situation would turn around. And it did. Mr.

Adams turned the words of the Crown's solicitor back on him and, in the end, the loggers went free.

♥

"How I wished Henry were home, too!" The words flew out of my mouth before I could stop them.

"As do I," Mother sighed. "The tavern is much quieter without him, don't you think?"

I had to smile. "Yes. It's been some time since we've heard the clatter of tankards and trenchers bouncing off the floor and the loud swearing of a customer drenched in beer."

Our mood would have been lighter had our dear Henry also been back in our fold. Last month, the Royal Navy impressed my third brother into service. And though we checked every incoming ship for correspondence, we'd had no word from him.

"Remember what Geoffrey said, that it's likely he wouldn't be able to write," Mother said.

I nodded, recalling that my beau, who held a position with the British Army, had cautioned us early on. "Yes, they'll be at sea for weeks at a time, and once he is in port, the boatswain will task a sailor to watch him closely until the boatswain's sure he won't run. After that, perhaps we'll hear from him."

Our hearts had soared at that tidbit of news, but it was difficult to keep our spirits buoyed as time passed. Henry has a quick mind and is perceptive to people and his surroundings. He's good with ciphering and is fleet-footed. Surely these traits would serve him well. More than anything, I needed to believe that he'd survive life aboard the *Hornet Sloop of War* and come home to Boston. I refused to believe otherwise.

♥

Little Christopher Snider is back at the tavern. The ten-year-old lad with blond hair and an impish grin sneaks in several times a day to pet and play with our dog, Boots. For his part, Boots is happy that somebody will pay attention to him, although in his old age, he finds it challenging to keep up with a human ball of energy.

Along the harbor, everyone knows Christopher. His fair face, smudged dark from street grime, and hands grubby from activities I don't care to know about, are his hallmark. He lives with and does chores for Mrs. Althorp, near Hancock Wharf, where his father works. His parents live on Frog Lane, on the southern end of Boston Common, far from the tavern. From time to time, the elder Snider and Eli load or unload a ship and later share an ale. His mother hires out her services, cleaning houses for the upper sort along Beacon Hill. Once he completes Mrs. Althorp's tasks, Christopher supervises his own days. That supervisory skill, however, needs to be honed. Days he should be in school, he spends elsewhere. Today, as has become his custom, he is visiting Boots.

"Miss Molly?"

The soprano voice reached me from behind the bar. I looked down to find Christopher crouched close to the wall and poking at something in the corner. Suddenly, I felt much older than my eighteen years, realizing I might have some disciplining to do.

"What's that you have?"

"I think it's a dead mouse. Where's Buttermilk? Wouldn't she like to have it for supper?"

Although I considered myself immune to the distasteful sight of my tabby eating rodents, I shuddered.

"No, Christopher, this one you will have to throw out yourself. Buttermilk eats only what she catches."

"That's too bad. This one would've made a good supper. Look at how fat he is!" His grubby fingers waved the gray creature by its tail so I could properly measure its size. He sighed, and to my surprise, slipped it into a pocket of his ragged pants. "I'll see whether any of the other cats wants it."

I wasn't sure that he'd find any takers for the diminutive carcass, but I did want him to leave The Three Lions with it. "Good idea. Then you can head over to school. You need to learn your lessons."

A long, deep sigh reached my ears as he trudged across the room. His mood bounced up when he reached the door. "See you tomorrow, Boots!"

The elderly dog raised his head at hearing his name, groaned, and laid his head on crossed paws. Within moments, he was snoring.

MARCH 1768

Eli Weston

Paul looked at me and, with a motion of his eyes, summoned me to follow. I watched as he entered the great room of The Three Lions and headed straight for the kitchen, tearing off his heavy coat and hat as he went. Geoffrey and I were sharing a mug of ale, but I excused myself to see what was on my brother's mind.

"You'll not believe what is being planned. Adams and Molineux are calling for the Sons to march on Burch's home." Paul topped off a full trencher with a generous slice of bread.

"Commissioner William Burch? Again? Surely you aren't serious! Haven't we enough to do with protecting ourselves against the raids? Why invite more attention by continuing to harass one of the customs officers?"

I rubbed my head and then worked my hands down my forehead and over my eyes. They reached my throat and then circled to the nape of my neck to massage the dull ache of oncoming tension. The new Board of Customs had installed five commissioners in late 1767—William Burch, Henry Hulton, Charles Paxton, John Robinson, and John Temple—men selected for their politics as well as their toadyish morals. A few of the Sons regularly paraded past the commissioners' homes. On occasion, they hurled epithets and heavier objects at the houses.

"Ah," Paul said, "but I know something you do not: Burch, Temple, and the others wrote to Commodore Hood a few weeks ago. They want government protection, and who better to provide that than the commodore and his flagship, the *HMS Romney*."

Paul's remark sent my mind reeling. If the request was sent two weeks ago, Boston could expect to see more soldiers and sailors within a month at the earliest. If Hood delayed his answer, well, then we wouldn't see troops for several months. The Sons would have to pull together a plan to counter the influx of British forces. The sooner we implement it, the better.

"Do Hancock and Adams know about the letter?"

"Not sure. I'm here to get some food in my belly, and then I'm off." He grabbed a trencher and slopped some gobbet stew into it, piled some biscuits on top, and sat down with a spoon.

"To join the others at Burch's?"

"What else? Those commissioners have taken to their positions like fleas to a dog. Time to make them as miserable as they're making us," he mumbled between shovelfuls of food.

"Make sure you aren't caught. We've enough to do. We can't afford you spending more time in jail."

"Don't worry, big brother. I think I've learned how to escape the lobsterbacks by now!"

I slapped him on the back for luck, then headed back to where I'd left Geoffrey and my ale.

As I approached the table, Geoffrey looked at me with questioning eyes. I told him nothing except "You'll hear soon enough. Trouble is brewing at Commissioner Burch's home."

"I see. Do I have time to eat my supper?"

♥

After Paul and I were released from jail, we didn't dare go back into the forests. Instead of logging, the two of us went to the wharves for work. Paul had developed a musculature most men would envy, and so my younger brother joined me as a dockworker. In the forest, he had been my overseer, but now our roles would reverse, and I would teach him the ways of the docks.

Today, however, most men had taken a holiday. It was the anniversary of the Stamp Act announcement, March 18, and, cold as it was, the city was preparing for a celebration.

"Eli, what time does he want us?" Paul's question snapped me out of my memories.

"What? Oh, right. Hancock said that after lunch is good. We'll need to pick up the streamers from Benjamin Church's warehouse first."

John Hancock had asked us to help him decorate his house on Beacon Street, facing Boston Common. Paul and I would drape the windows with red and blue streamers. Other friends were tasked with setting up a cask of Madeira in the front yard, and others had been assigned to serve the wine to the celebrants.

We had loaded a cart with yards of material and reached the Common when we heard shouting. A bit of a rumpus had broken out. Several men had hung effigies—of whom we weren't sure—but our instinct told us they were of Andrew Oliver and Thomas Hutchinson—the infamous cronies at the root of all the Stamp Act nonsense from three years ago.

"Hey, there! Stop that!"

I pushed and shoved my way through the small, but growing, crowd to reach Liberty Tree. Two young lads, maybe fifteen years old, poked at the figures with pointed sticks.

"Get on home! Go on!"

Paul and I shooed the boys away, disassembled the crude gibbets, and the effigies fell to the snow-covered ground. Rather than Oliver and Hutchinson, however, likenesses of Commissioner Paxton and Inspector Williams looked up at us.

I turned to address the crowd that had gathered.

"Today is a day to celebrate the repeal of this heinous act," I began. "Let's not use it as a way to destroy our city. We must unite as one mind to celebrate with the Crown that, in its wisdom, realized the injustice of the Stamp Act. Today, we shouldn't demonstrate against it. Let's demonstrate our support of Parliament's decision to repeal it."

♥

After Paul and I had sent the miscreants home from the Liberty Tree, we hauled the effigies into the cart and circled west to Hancock's house. A dozen workers swarmed the yard and building to make the stately home even more fancy.

One of the women servants monitored our efforts as we draped lengths of red and blue fabric out each window.

Her shrill voice directed us. "Not so much! Don't let it drag on the ground! Higher! Pull it higher!"

"Could she be any more particular?" muttered Paul. "I don't see much reason to keep adjusting the length when it's going to be dark soon, and nobody's going to notice one inch either way."

"Hush! That's her way of managing those she feels superior to."

"We're not her lackeys!"

"Quiet down! She'll hear you!"

"I don't care!"

"Well, you should care. For some people, well, they just need to feel they are better than others. How did you feel when you were able to go into the forest, but Henry had to stay behind? Didn't you feel like you were better than him?"

Paul grumbled. "A bit."

"That's part of what the riots were about—we didn't want Parliament telling us what to do without our approval. If we had the right to speak and be heard, we might not have had those riots in '65. The Body of the People was formed so that everyone could lay a claim to our actions."

"But that voice! Any more of it and the sound of her voice will pierce my ears!"

We both laughed and finished up quickly.

Later that night, Paul and I enjoyed the festivities at the British Coffee House with about fifty other men. Lots of the Irish were in the establishment, and we consecrated the holiday with toasts to the King and Queen, friends of America, and the Pennsylvania Farmer, John Dickinson. Once our tongues were loosed, toasts were called out for the *Boston-Gazette* and those who vindicated the freedom of the press. Someone dedicated his drink to the success of the American manufactories now underway. And one of the Irish, feeling particularly tipsy, thought we should also toast St. Patrick.

Worried that the drinkers might get too disorderly, I urged them: "Fellows, before we get too unsteady, let's pledge to keep the peace this evening. Come, let's patrol."[2]

GEOFFREY CANFIELD

Boston was celebrating once again. They celebrated as soon as they learned the Stamp Act had been repealed, and then they celebrated again several months later. Now, two years after the fact, there is another festival in progress. I shook my head in disbelief. This city, these people, found every reason to enjoy life, even in the midst of difficulty.

As I dressed, I heard a scratching sound at my door. Buttermilk, Molly's yellow tabby, had somehow been relegated to spending the night in the hallway, or wherever she slept when she wasn't sprawled across my bed. Why she needed to be inside my room now, I would never understand. She raced inside and jumped onto my table, sending my brush, powder, and wig flying across the room.

"Egad, cat!" I tried to brush her off the table, but she had somehow grown leaden. The cat wouldn't budge.

"For goodness' sake!" I gathered my scattered belongings and placed them on the bed. The cat, by now, had sprawled across the table and occupied every inch while she attended to her toilette.

I sat on the side of the bed, combed the wig into proper form, and fitted it on my head. Tonight, I would be celebrating with Molly, and I wanted to look my best.

♥

The closer we came to Beacon Street and the Common, the heavier the crowds. Soon, Molly and I were carried along with the flow toward the snowy grounds. The occasional cannon fire roared in our ears, and with each salvo, the crowd erupted into huzzahs and toasts.

Eventually, we made our way to the Hancock house. The lawn had become a slushy, muddy, and ruddy mess from all the connoisseurs of Madeira who loitered around the cask. Molly delicately picked her way through the crowd, carefully scanning the ground for the least trodden sections, and once we reached the front steps, sighed audibly.

"I didn't think we'd make it!" She laughed, but then began to laugh even harder. "But it looks as if your breeches will need some extra scrubbing!"

I looked to where she pointed. Brown slush had whimsically splattered the lower portion of the trousers.

"Perhaps my wit will keep everyone from looking at my legs." At which Molly laughed once more.

"Come, let's see how you fare in conversation," she answered gaily and grabbed my hand, pulling me up the steps and through the front door.

Our host, John Hancock, gently clasped Molly's hand in greeting and slightly bowed.

"Lieutenant Canfield. Welcome to my home." Hancock shook my hand and, with his left hand on my back, led me away from Molly, who was already in conversation with Mercy Warren.

"William Burch has written to Governor Bernard."

"A complaint about the demonstration at his house?"

"Not simply a complaint, Geoffrey. He asked Bernard to write for more troops to be sent to Boston for protection."

"Bernard would have to petition General Gage in New York. I'm not sure Gage will honor such an individual request."

"That was my thought, too. Although after today's mischief on the Common, there may be another request."

"Mischief?"

"Some of the lads swung Paxton and Williams in effigy from Liberty Tree."

I exhaled sharply.

Commissioner Charles Paxton worked for the Board of Customs, although the word *work* may have been a misnomer. He relished the position for the power it gave him over Boston's merchants, and he used that power for personal gain.

"You think Paxton will petition for troops as well?" I asked.

"Well, Burch already has. His petition was sent out late this afternoon to Commander Samuel Hood. He asked not only for troops, but also that the warship *Romney* be sent."

"Because he swung in effigy?"

"Not only that, but he claims he fears for his life as well as that of his family."

"Perhaps he should reconsider his position if he is so frightened. Come, let's enjoy the celebration."

April 1768

GEOFFREY CANFIELD

I never knew what to expect from my superior, General Bridgewater. His imperious demeanor and seemingly irrational demands made every man under his command flinch under his stare. When he wasn't parading us around Boston Common practicing maneuvers, he belted out useless orders for springtime Boston.

"Polish those boots!"

"Shine those buttons!"

Though I appreciated the idea of a well-dressed army and that maintaining our uniforms upheld discipline, keeping our footwear clean was a never-ending battle. While on patrol, we trekked through muck-ridden streets for hours at a time. Pig, cow, and horse dung mixed with mud to become a mucilaginous mire that dried hard as bricks on every surface. Carts drawn by oxen and horses sprayed the brownish sludge onto everything, including our white breeches. Salty air pitted brass so deeply that a gleaming button or buckle, though an admirable goal, was well-nigh impossible after a soldier had been stationed in this port city for several months.

Every night we chipped away at the mud-riddled boots and rubbed at our coat buttons till our fingers were raw. White breeches grayed with time, regardless of the efforts of our landladies to brighten them.

After Eli and I had destroyed Bridgewater's cache of black powder at the Mill in Dorchester, I walked a fine line with my commander. Shortly afterward, he seemed oblivious to my involvement, but over the last couple of months, I've perceived a change in his demeanor. His beady stare follows me from daily informational meetings to the taverns and even to social affairs. Even when he isn't around, I feel his eyes drilling into my back. Of course, that's ridiculous, yet these days, I frequently find myself shaking my shoulders as if to cast off the feeling. I could never be sure that Jack and Salmon hadn't passed on to Bridgewater the role Eli and I had played in the explosion before those two scoundrels escaped to the western frontier. Then there is my concern about Molly's friend Hester; more than once, I've found myself grinding my jaw while thinking of that woman.

I needed to clear the fog of uncertainty if I were to continue working with the Sons of Liberty. Should the general learn of my involvement with the group, then my fate would be sealed, and a gibbet would be etched with my name. Permanently. If he didn't know, then my path toward freedom and a future in America would be possible.

One afternoon at the wharf, I grabbed several customs invoices and managed to find Eli on the pretense of discussing the cargo of the latest ship to dock.

"What have you heard from Cotton?"

"Nothing. Since I told him about you and Molly, he's taken to drinking over on King Street."

"We need to get close to him again. What do you think about having Cotton follow the general? He did well enough with Matthew."

Matthew had been in service to Lt. Governor Thomas Hutchinson on Castle Island. We'd taken him into our confidence, and he and Cotton spied on the general's crew to intercept Bridgewater's illegal black powder ring. Unbeknownst to us, Matthew served only his master and betrayed our efforts, leading to Molly's capture and near death when the powder kegs caught fire and exploded, burning the mill to the ground.

"I suppose I could get Cotton to drink elsewhere," Eli said. "He is as yet unknown to Bridgewater, so he can roam more freely than you or I. What will be difficult, as you know, will be to convince him to come back to The Three Lions. The tavern could spare the extra pennies to fund his subterfuge; perhaps that will be enough incentive."

"Surely, he doesn't still bear me animosity for losing Molly. He never had her love to lose!"

"Ah, but as I recall, you resented the time they spent together."

"With good reason! Molly and I had an understanding when he rushed out of the dark and swept her off her feet."

"Geoffrey, we can go around and around on this, but let's set the matter aside. Molly's affection is with you, and Cotton has made himself scarce, which to me indicates he has deferred to you and your relationship. Wouldn't you agree?"

With a sigh, I nodded, and we decided that Cotton should further develop his reconnaissance skills by frequenting the taverns on King Street. Eli left my room to find Cotton and win him back to our efforts.

As I snuffed the last candle at my bedside that night, a niggling thought about Eli's friend interrupted my path to sleep. He had so quickly and easily befriended Matthew, and Matthew so convincingly demonstrated his loyalty to our cause, only to show his true Tory colors by capturing my Molly. Could Cotton be as Matthew, a traitor to our cause?

Since that night, Molly and I rekindled our romance, and we were on a path to building a future together, navigating a path strewn with rocks and debris, but progress was slow.

I sighed and shook my head. For a time, I thought my Molly was lost to me. Cotton strolled into the space between us, and she responded. Thinking of them together renewed the anger that I previously tamped down. Shall I ever get over this jealousy? Cotton proved his loyalty by freeing Molly, and he recently acknowledged the relationship Molly and I share.

I rubbed my eyes, trying to erase Cotton's image from my vision. Trust needed to be earned, but this time, we didn't have time for Cotton to gain it back. I needed to rely on him because the one man in Boston I knew I could never have faith in General Emory Bridgewater.

Hester Winslow

"You need to get closer to that tavern girl," he said.

Although I was concentrating on the blemished maple tabletop, I couldn't help but roll my eyes and sigh. My index finger drew a semicircle around the base of my cup as I struggled to maintain my composure. This was not what I wanted to hear from General Bridgewater.

Our three o'clock rendezvous at the Alderton Coffee House exhausted me. Worn tables, singed hearths, and smudged walls mirrored my dark demeanor. I'd ordered my second beverage by the time he arrived, which prickled my pride. A lady should not be kept waiting! The Alderton specialized in serving British officers and Loyalists; that is, the owner had an unimaginable cache of tea stored off-site that he brewed for his clients. The coffee house had quickly become the general's favorite meeting place—their fondness for serving an item from the boycott list outweighed their lack of adornment in his eyes. But not in mine. The sole embellishment in this so-called coffee house was an unrefined portrait of King George III that hung over the fireplace.

"If she and Lieutenant Canfield are behind the destruction of my powder, then I must have more details. You allege that my lieutenant colludes with these rebels. You claim to have a source. Why don't I have details, facts? Why don't I know who you are talking to? Prove to me that he did it. Innuendo isn't enough, madam. I need to know everything. Get me the information I need to court-martial that blackguard!"

I looked beyond his shoulder and scanned the dim room, searching for anyone who might save me from the verbal abuse spewing my way. I wasn't accustomed to being spoken to in such a harsh manner. All the patrons, however, paid attention only to their drinks. Nary a glance came my way. *He should save that tone for his troops, not me!*

"Are you listening?"

The louder tone startled me. "Of course," I stammered, "you want specifics."

General Bridgewater narrowed his eyes and leaned across the small table. "The sooner the better. It's already been several months, and you have nothing to show. If you want to better your position, bring me proof!"

The pompous British officer rose to his feet. Seated patrons ducked and protected their drinks as he plowed his way through the field of tables to the doorway.

I wasn't sure what to do. My cheeks burned from the encounter, both from the tongue-lashing as well as being left alone, still seated, in a public place. No gentleman would ever leave a lady in such fashion. The man could use a lesson in manners!

Fortunately, there was still a bit of tea in my cup. With a smile on my lips, I raised the cup and sipped. I nodded to a woman staring at me, my smile signaling that I'd meant to remain at the table, and those few moments saved my reputation. They also gave me time to calm my nerves as I pondered how to win back Molly's confidence.

Unfortunately, over the past year, some of our interactions had challenged our friendship. Although I wasn't bothered that some of the fault lay with me, I wondered if there were still a way to win back that girl's trust. Cyrus has always complimented me on my depth of resourcefulness. Now will be the time to fully implement it.

Cotton Easton

Blame it! Here she comes. That woman is more of a jade than I thought possible. I pity the devil who married the harridan.

I'd glanced back but wasn't quick enough to escape her notice.

"Cotton! Cotton!" The shrill voice carried from across the street, and manners dictated that I delay my travel. She gently placed her hand on my forearm and acted as if our chance encounter were anything but.

"It's good of you to come," she said, at which my left eyebrow cocked inadvertently.

I bowed slightly in greeting. "Of course, Goody Winslow." The abbreviated term *Goodwife* stuck in my throat. Hester's intentions could never be construed as good.

Her lips curled gently into a smile that months ago I'd have enjoyed seeing on her beautiful face. Too many encounters with her, however, showed me her deviousness. Nowadays, all I see in that smile is wicked intent.

"What pleases you today?" I asked.

"Pleases me?"

Her laughter rang hollow, and much like a guard dog, my hackles rose, anticipating the yet unseen menace.

The sweet and coquettish voice returned. "I have something to say that will very much please you. Walk with me."

Hester never asked; she commanded. Yet the topic of conversation perplexed me. It wasn't in concert with the urgency of her tone, nor was it one I would have selected. As we walked, she prattled on about her latest clothing purchase—a blue petticoat she bought at Anna's shop. The only interesting item in her discourse was the mention of where Molly worked. But as she talked and talked, I realized she didn't share my preoccupation with Molly. My mind wandered during the one-sided conversation till I realized she had smoothly guided us to the Common, where so many soldiers camp. *Amongst so many redcoats, she must feel safe. Nobody here to betray her.*

Hester's voice dropped a notch, and her flirtatious nature vanished. *Now I'll find out why she's here.* "The general needs your help."

"That's difficult to believe. He has hundreds of men under his command. It's unlikely anything I could do would be of merit."

"You think too little of your worth. It's who you know that makes you valuable, Cotton. Let's combine your knowledge with my cunning. General Bridgewater promised to make it profitable for both of us."

"If there is a way to benefit, then I'd best yield to your wishes." I inclined my head slightly and silently hoped for easy and quick returns on my knowledge. *But please don't let it be about Molly.*

Hester Winslow

Poor Cotton. He's like a lost lamb looking for a shepherd. Well, in this case, a shepherdess.

"You see, my dear fellow, it's time to recoup some of our, er, your losses."

I looped my hand back through his arm and steered him toward a bench at the edge of the Common, a bit further from the tents and parading soldiers and the dust they stirred up while marching. Boston's grazing cattle had long since been corralled off their pasture, and the soldiers' continual drilling killed off any remaining greenery. I coughed behind my fan and tried to ventilate the air in front of my face.

I sat down and indicated with my hand that Cotton should follow suit. I smoothed my petticoat and broached the subject that General Bridgewater demanded. Facts. Details. Proof.

"You are in a unique position," I began. "You spent all that time with Eli and Lt. Canfield. Not to mention Matthew."

"No! You won't get me to say anything against them."

"Come now, Cotton. How good a friend sends you to get jailed? I don't think I could ever do anything like that to one of my dearest companions."

The tall blond rubbed his hands up and down his thighs so fiercely that I could distinguish the directions. His eyes were open, but he didn't see the regulars drilling on the Common.

Quick movement across the grounds caught my attention. A smallish figure, half the size of a Regular, was darting in and out of the drilling platoons. The curly blond-haired boy looked familiar, but I couldn't immediately place him in my mind's list of acquaintances. I turned my attention back to the tall blond in front of me.

"They let you get captured, and then they leave you to rot in that jail!"

"But it wasn't like that."

"It was! How long were you held? And once you were out, they forced you to spy on the mill."

He was remembering—the frigid November temperatures, the hunger, the hours of tedium. His eyes refocused, and I could see that we shared the same view.

"What do you want from me?" he growled.

"Nothing much really, just the whole story of the black powder plot. The general just needs a few details. What you did, who you talked to, that sort of thing."

"Information like that could have me swinging from the gibbet!"

"Oh, don't be silly! By giving him the information, you're implicating the others, not yourself. The general needs you. Remember, you're valuable because of this information. Besides, he has promised us compensation."

Cotton abruptly stood and began to pace in front of the bench. He clenched and unclenched his fists, and dirt swirled upwards as he strode back and forth. I needed him to turn on his friends; my relationship with Molly was shaky, and I may not be able to repair it quickly enough to get what the general's demanded. My mind willed him to do my bidding.

Cotton Easton

This woman is driving me mad!

I had to keep pacing until I had an answer for Hester. Thoughts chased one another through my head. So much was happening! To turn in Eli and Geoffrey meant Bridgewater still didn't know what happened at the mill. I'll admit that making a pal of the lieutenant governor's manservant was useful, but Matthew played us against one another as much as he helped. That Bridgewater didn't know who had blown up his cache was only because Matthew'd suffered a head wound during the explosion.

"Shh!" I hushed Hester as she tried to interrupt my thoughts.

I watched my feet as I paced, and the rhythm soothed the chaos in my head. *No matter what she says, once I tell Bridgewater what happened, there is no certainty that he won't also charge me with the plot. I need a way to incriminate them while I remain blame-free. And once Canfield is gone, Molly will have to come back to me.*

I stopped and stood up straight. A smile inched across my face, and I turned to my lady companion.

As I stretched out my hand to assist her in standing, she asked, "Well? Have we reached a bargain?"

"Yes, madam, we have." *But it may not be the bargain you expect.*

May 1768

Eli Weston

The Board of Customs, comprised of Henry Hulton, Charles Paxton, William Burch, John Robinson, and John Temple, repeatedly wrote to Commodore Hood in Halifax requesting protection from Boston's citizens. They reacted to the demonstrations by increasing the number of searches conducted on ships and warehouses, but when they asked the governor to request troops on their behalf, it was no longer an empty threat. The Sons of Liberty would not be intimidated. Nevertheless, I kept an eye out for troop movements. My concern was reinforced when the Man o' War *HMS Romney* sailed into Boston Harbor with a regiment of eighty soldiers in addition to its complement of seamen on May 17.

From Long Wharf, Paul and I watched Captain Jack Corner pilot the *Romney*. She was a formidable sight with a flourish of sailors standing at attention along her prow, her fifty guns gleaming in the sun, and the red, white, and blue Union Flag waving briskly. To my surprise, she wasn't alone. The *HMS St. Lawrence*, a schooner of ten guns, escorted the *Romney*.

"Sends a shiver down your spine, doesn't it?" Paul commented under his breath.

"With that many guns, it looks to me as if they're expecting to do more than protect families."

The *Romney* and the *St. Lawrence* moored off Castle Island, their presence an ominous reminder that England was keeping a close eye on the Massachusetts Bay Colony.

The British Army wasted no time. Regiments took possession of Castle William and began repairs to its battlements.

More and more people frequented the wharves to watch the construction across the harbor. Tavern gossip darkened. Nobody strengthens an aging fortress unless there are plans for its future use.

"Watch yourself," Paul cautioned me as I folded my work apron.

"What aren't you telling me?"

"Nobody's heard from Saul. Two days now. They think he was impressed."

After Henry's disappearance last winter, the press gangs had quieted down. We hadn't learned of other impressments in many months, but worried that more would occur once the *Romney* landed.

Keeping my brother's warning in mind, I stealthily headed for the Green Dragon.

June 1768

Geoffrey Canfield

In the six months since patriots had paraded his effigy in the Pope's Night festivities, Commissioner Paxton had redoubled his efforts to ferret out smuggling activity. Working under another commissioner, William Burch, he and his tidesmen routinely boarded sloops and merchant ships to compare bills of lading with actual cargo. The more smuggled goods the men confiscated, the fatter Paxton's purse. He claimed one-third of the seized goods; the remaining two-thirds were split between the province and the governor—all the more reason for Governor Bernard to support Paxton and his tidesmen. And double the reasons for merchants to be wary.

On June 10, General Bridgewater ordered me to Long Wharf.

I didn't know what required our presence, but disturbances along the wharves broke out regularly. The noise grew louder as we neared the moorings of John Hancock's sloop, *Liberty*, where dock workers hurled stones and curses at a small crew of tidesmen.

"Go back to England!"

"Scurvy rats!"

"Board your own boat and drown!"

British Navy midshipmen William Senhouse, William Culmer, and Walter Booth had boarded the sloop, forcibly removed, with muskets and clubs, the men off the boat, and untied its moorings. Now afloat, they ducked the missiles as they towed the *Liberty* out to the man o' war *Romney*.

The stones didn't hinder the tidesmen from completing their duty, yet the mob's anger still needed a release. The workers turned from the sea in search of a scapegoat. Homes of one or more of the commissioners would be a logical choice. During the Stamp Act riots, Charles Paxton saved his house by pleading with the riotous mob. Since then, his proclivity to mandate searches of boats, warehouses, and homes, oftentimes baseless, discredited his reputation. My heart skipped a beat thinking about the coming destruction.

"Keep back!" I shouted to the crowd.

"Hold the line!" to my men.

The workers pressed against the patrol, and my men pushed back. In the distance, Billy Culmer stood in the *Liberty*, his gun aimed at the crowd. Culmer, known among his fellow sailors to be a blood thirsty madman, would be itching to fire. I quickly clambered atop a crate to calm the impassioned workers.

"I know you're angry," I began.

"Angry? We'll show you angry!" The crowd surged toward the line of redcoats. The soldiers held their guns horizontally and pushed back. Bloodshed loomed in my mind.

I tried again. "Restrain yourselves. No good can come of more violence. You've landed some good-sized stones on the tidesmen—they'll be hurting come morning."

"They have Hancock's sloop."

"They do, but let Mr. Hancock sort it out with the commissioners."

"He'll get it back, you know. We'll make sure of it."

"Yes, he probably will."

I nodded to the workers and jumped off the makeshift dais, signaling to the crowd to disperse as well.

The crowd left the harbor, but made its way toward the homes of the customs agents, where their stones and bricks found purchase in more windows. So severe were the attacks that the families fled to the *Romney,* which ferried them to Castle William under Navy guard.

That evening, I mulled over the day's events. Hancock would surely get the *Liberty* returned to him. It may take a week or longer, but the government couldn't move against a man of his stature in the community without expecting repercussions. John Hancock's holdings ranged from shipbuilding and ropewalks to importing and exporting goods as well as warehousing them. He operated the entire line of commerce, and he paid his men well. But will they fight for him? Today's events made me think Hancock's hirelings would willingly take up arms for him.

Molly Weston

"Who is this Hannah Griffitts?" I asked Eli.

It was early in the morning, and we were drinking coffee, waiting for the rest of the household to wake up. I had been fussing with the previous day's *Gazette* and came across a long poem written by a Daughter of Liberty, or so she said. The name was unfamiliar to me, and these days, I doubted more than I trusted anyone I didn't know.

"You remember the Pennsylvania Farmer? They are related."

"Must be through marriage. Dickinson and Griffitts are hardly the same name."

"Just as your name will change when you marry," he retorted and then quickly winked.

I refused to be baited, so I switched the topic.

"She must be well informed, as she talks about each of the taxes in the Townshend Acts."

"Let me see that." Eli grabbed the newspaper. He scanned the poem for a few moments.

THE FEMALE PATRIOTS.
ADDRESSED TO THE DAUGHTERS OF
LIBERTY IN AMERICA.
BY THE SAME

Since the Men from a Party, or fear of a Frown,
Are kept by a Sugar-Plumb, quiety down.
Supinely asleep, & depriv'd of their Sight
Are strip'd of their Freedom, & rob'd of their Right.
If the Son (so degenerate) the Blessing despise,
Let the Daughters of Liberty, nobly arise,
And tho' we've no Voice, but a negative here.
The use of the Taxables, let us forebear,
(Then Merchants import till yr. Stores are all full
May the Buyers be few & yr. Traffick be dull.)
Stand firmly resolved & bid Grenville to see
That rather than Freedom, we'll part with our Tea

And well as we love the dear Draught when a dry,
As American Patriots,—our Taste we deny,
Sylvania's, gay Meadows, can richly afford,
To pamper our Fancy, or furnish our Board,
And Paper sufficient (at home) still we have,
To assure the Wise-acre, we will not sign Slave.
When this Homespun shall fail, to remonstrate our Grief
We can speak with the Tongue or scratch on a Leaf.
Refuse all their Colours, tho richest of Dye,
The juice of a Berry—our Paint can supply,
To humour our Fancy—& as for our Houses,
They'll do without painting as well as our Spouses,
While to keep out the Cold of a keen winter Morn
We can screen the Northwest, with a well polish'd Horn,
And trust me a Woman by honest Invention
Might give this State Doctor a Dose of Prevention.
Join mutual in this, & but small as it seems
We may Jostle a Grenville & puzzle his Schemes
But a motive more worthy our patriot Pen,
Thus acting—we point out their Duty to Men,
And should the bound Pensioners, tell us to hush
We can throw back the Satire by biding them blush.
by Hannah Griffitts[3]

"She is knowledgeable about the taxes," he said. "She mentions them all: tea, paper, dyes, glass. Did you see that part about wearing homespun?"

"Yes." I tapped my fingers on the table and thought for a moment. "Mother and Anna are still trying to put together a spinning contest. Perhaps we can use this poem to encourage the women to enlist."

"A Battle of Thread?" Eli teased. "Don't roll your eyes."

"You make it difficult to be serious, brother. What we ladies do for Boston, we do for you."

He rose and planted a kiss on my forehead. "We men know of your efforts. You *are* appreciated."

Eli Weston

Out of the corner of my eye, I could see a slight commotion at the far end of Long Wharf. Daniel Malcolm rushed the length of the dock, dodging workers loading crates and bundles, knocking over a couple of men and boxes as he approached.

"Come quickly," he panted. "Tidesmen are making their way toward Hancock Wharf. I fear they'll board the *Lydia*."

Knowing that Hancock had caught the eye of the commissioners, Daniel Malcolm and I took turns keeping watch on the Hancock ships and his wharf. Hancock's sloop, *Lydia*, had arrived from the West Indies and likely held a cargo of Madeira wine. Hancock had purchased his own wharf to avoid the prying eyes of customs.

The reason for the purchase, however, wasn't lost on the commissioners. The businessman had publicly scorned the newly instituted American Board of Commissioners by refusing to attend their inaugural reception. We didn't know whether his absence was due to the earlier raid on his warehouse or simply because he disagreed with Parliament's establishment of the American Board of Commissioners to oversee new customs regulations and merchant ships. He never said.

Of course, everyone in Boston knew the history of Thomas Hancock and his smuggling activities. The elder Hancock spent his career bringing in wine, rum, molasses, and spices to the colonies under the cover of night. As his wealth grew, he built one of the largest and most beautiful houses along the Common. He shared his largesse with the citizens, his final gift consisting of £600 to the city for a new poorhouse. Many of the upper sort believed that his nephew John had continued the family practice of smuggling. That information, however, we patriots kept from nosy customs officers. If the officers were making their way to the *Lydia*, I had to question whether someone had slipped information to the Board of Commissioners.

"Get McKay and Hancock right away. I'll meet you there."

Malcolm was right. By the time we reached the *Lydia*, tidesmen had already boarded.

We lined up behind Hancock, who was already on board and livid. "Show me the warrants! You may not search before I see the warrants!"

Hancock's assertiveness flustered the tidesman in charge.

"I, uh, well, I don't have any papers."

"You don't have a warrant!" Hancock bellowed, advancing on the officer. "You dare to search my ship, and you don't have a warrant? Get off! Get off my ship!"

The tidesman backed away from the diminutive but determined man and disembarked with his officers.

Molly Weston

"We should do something about that boy," I overheard Father tell Mother. "He needs looking after." They were talking about Christopher Snider.

"But he's too young to work in the tavern, Jonathan."

Father ignored his wife's opinion. "His parents set a good example for work, but they've sent him over to Grizzell Althorp's, and it's time somebody stepped in. I don't think Goody Althorp is encouraging a proper work ethic. Mind you, I'm not taking him in as an apprentice; you're right that he's too young for that. But we could do something to instill a bit of responsibility. He spends enough time here; we might as well teach him something."

I warmed to the idea of having young Christopher around and stepped into the conversation. "He's grown a bit since we've been feeding him, Father, so perhaps he could help out in the tavern with smaller tasks. Clear trenchers, tankards from the tables, and such."

"Molly, that's a wonderful idea," Mother said. "It's a small enough task, but one that needs doing, especially since Henry is gone. I could even use Christopher in the kitchen washing up."

Father stood. "Then that's what we'll do. I'll find my way over to the wharf and talk to his father this afternoon."

It's official. Christopher Snider now works part-time at The Three Lions. He makes his first appearance of the day just as we're finishing lunch. Mother feeds him biscuits and coffee, and then, once he's cleared the tables in the general room, she shoos him out the door to attend his afternoon lessons. Rather than returning home after class or wandering the wharves scouting for mischief, he comes back to the tavern and takes his orders from Paul till returning to Mrs. Althorp's in the evening.

"Boy! Not like—"

A deafening crash interrupted him. Mugs bounced off the table and clanged along the floor. Men jumped from the benches, reaching down to wipe ale from their breeches and shoes.

I grabbed towels and dashed to the table where Christopher had dropped his tray.

♥

Father's efforts to teach Christopher basic tavern skills, such as making beer, so he would be able to make a living once grown, were delayed. Instead, Mother took him under her apron strings, spending time to improve his grammar and manners, which softened Christopher's rough edges. Henry is still missing, and even though he cannot replace my brother, young Chris eases Mother's loss, making her smile with his willingness to please.

He makes me smile too. And for the first time in months, I am happy to have the hole Henry left in my heart being filled.

July 1768

Eli Weston

I sipped at my beer and grimaced. The stifling heat and humidity had permeated the dark interior of the Three Lions, raising the temperature of everything that should be cool, from drink to mood. Seemed the warmer the beer, the hotter the drinkers' ire.

Watching Paxton's purse grow thick off the backs of merchants stirred my anger even more. Just remembering Senhouse and Culmer gleefully bludgeoning anyone in their way… I had to shake my head to clear it of the dark thoughts tumbling through.

"Eli!" I turned my head toward the shout.

Paul was headed my way, carrying a tankard of ale in each hand. Cooler than the one I had now, I hoped.

"I have an idea," he said as he hefted a leg over the bench. "What if we began to focus on something different?"

"That's quite a cryptic way to begin a conversation, brother."

"Just that I've been thinking about the *Liberty* and all the other ships and merchants who've been raided by the tidesmen. What if we turned the tide on the tidesmen?"

I threw my head back and laughed while Paul's eyes widened in surprise. "What's so funny?"

"If you only knew what I have just been thinking about!"

August 1768

Geoffrey Canfield

The summer heat has been brutal. No sooner had I entered my quarters than I unbuttoned that scarlet woolen atrocity of a coat and rolled up my sleeves. Splashing water on my face and neck helped to cool me, but for a moment, at least, the dust was washed away.

Today's post brought another letter from my father. I'll have to talk to Molly about the epistle, as there will be no way to keep the news from her. And Ben Edes, that intrepid journalist, will be sure to publish something about whatever its contents are before long. I sat on the corner of the bed, hoping to be the first to learn of the situation in Britain.

John Wilkes, publisher of *The North Briton*, dared to republish the infamous article from issue 45 that had caused all his troubles several years ago. No sooner did he return from self-exile in France than the Crown jailed him for treason at King's Bench Prison in Southwark.

Wilkes, through correspondence and visits from supporters—even those Americans abroad—has maintained, and possibly increased, the call for his release. Here in Boston, the Sons of Liberty, including Eli and Henry, were behind the surreptitious appearances of the number 45 on doors and windows.

> It is estimated that 15,000 people gathered in St. George's Fields, outside King's Bench Prison, on May 10. Their purpose was to show support for the libertine Scot, but as is wont to happen, a few began their belligerent behavior shouting slogans: "Wilkes and Liberty! No Liberty, No King!" The most egregious of them shouted "Damn the King! Damn the Government! Damn the Justices!"
>
> My son, such treasonous behavior could not go unanswered by the Royal Guard! As you might expect, the Horse Grenadier Guards were dispatched to subdue the crowd. They found one of the ringleaders and chased

him into a barn. They knew him from his red coat. In the midst of the ensuing chaos, some of the grenadiers chased another man, also in a red coat, firing upon and killed him.

Subsequently, the agitators grew even more riotous, and the Third Regiment of Foot Guards was called to join with the Grenadiers in putting down the masses. More shots were fired, and at last report, 11 persons lost their life that day. Up to 15 more were seriously injured.

Even more damaging, because it affects the country overall, individuals who weren't involved in the St. George's Fields melee championed the rioters: sawyers destroyed the sawmills where they worked, sailors unrigged outbound ships, and even watermen ruined private boats and threatened to destroy bridges.

These are just examples of what transpired, Geoffrey, and as you can imagine, the King himself was disheartened by the extent of the destruction. He was so demoralized by these acts of civil disobedience that more than one peer spoke of his pending abdication.

Father's letter caused me to think about the ramifications of the St. George's massacre. If more British were siding with Wilkes against the Crown, well, that would have to indicate a change of heart in Parliament towards America.

Molly Weston

The number 45 was at eye level as I opened the door to Anna's shop. Eli hadn't mentioned that he had gone out to scratch numerals in doorframes last night, but I wished he had skipped Anna's. He knows she is with us.

"You've seen our newest sign?" Anna called out from the back of the shop.

"I apologize for my brother and his friends."

"Don't worry about it. I was beginning to think it was more conspicuous not to have the number on the shop. This way, we are just one of many visited by the long-reaching pen of John Wilkes. We disappear into the woodwork!"

"Wilkes and Liberty!" I whispered under my breath.

Anna leaned in. "Yes, Wilkes and Liberty!"

♥

"I said, 'Good afternoon!'"

"Oh, my! How may I help you, ma'am?" The words instinctively tumbled forth as I rushed to put away my latest effort at writing an advice for the *Gazette*.

"Oh!" I couldn't keep from gasping when I looked up to see Hester standing but a foot away.

"Don't look so surprised to see me, Molly. You know that Anna has the best selections in women's clothing."

"It's just been so long since you've made a purchase here."

"Yes, well," Hester paused as she breathed deeply. "Well, I have tried to shop at Jane Eustis's, but the quality is missing. I don't know what's become of her lately; she's still trying to sell off last year's fashions."

Poor Jane. Her health had been suffering ever since her husband left for another woman, and she petitioned the courts for a divorce decree. Divorce was more common than it had been, but still. I shuddered at imagining the frail woman suffering under Hester's complaints. And if Hester had noticed that Jane wasn't restocking her wares, she would certainly detect that our shelves were filled with homespun items and not the shimmering silks and satins from Europe. My head bowed, inadvertently awaiting the grievances sure to leave her mouth.

"Please show me your mantuas. My own outer garment has suffered several rips recently, and my maid cannot see her way to mend them properly."

"Yes, of course." *Poor maid. Another soul tormented by Hester. That woman could easily mend the mantua; she's always talking about how beautifully she sews.*

"This is a lovely color." Hester was fingering a blue linen garment. If her fingers had perceived it was homespun, she didn't let me know.

"Help me put it on."

After several twirls and a lingering inspection of the seams and hem, Hester announced she would make the purchase.

"That was a surprise," Anna later commented on the sale.

"Hester buying something from us?"

"Oh, no," Anna chuckled. "Hester being sociable, even friendly. If I didn't know her as well as I do, I'd say she was up to something."

"Wouldn't it be wonderful if she had truly turned over a leaf? Let's look forward and mark today as a start for her new journey."

"If that girl can change, well, let's see where she takes us."

September 1768

Eli Weston

I found Cotton some six blocks away at the Green Dragon, lean-ing on the bar with a mug of ale at his elbow. The tavern's din was such that quiet conversation was impossible. I clapped my friend on the back.

"Cotton!"

His eyes widened in surprise, and he greeted me with a smile that reached from ear to ear.

"Straying from The Lions again?"

"Only to find a missing friend. What say you to a walk?"

He hesitated a second before answering. A slight tightening around his eyes caught my attention and warned me to be alert.

"Sure. Let's head out." His eyes scanned the room. "But first..."

He grabbed his mug and emptied it in one long draught. He slammed the emptied tankard onto the counter, wiped his mouth on his sleeve, then turned to me and winked.

"Now, we can go."

Cotton's sharply honed behavior contrasted greatly with the easygoing personality I knew so well. *Is it possible for a friend to have changed so much so quickly?*

I pushed that thought aside, telling myself that he was still hurting from Molly's rejection. *If we didn't need him, I'd let him wallow in his grief.* I quickly scanned our options to employ other Sons of Liberty, but everyone had their hands full these days. *Cotton's tortured soul will have to wait to enjoy its misery.*

"Where have you been working?"

"Thought I'd try my hand at the ropewalk. Loading cargo and felling trees isn't much of an option these days."

I half chuckled at his description of work. Cotton had been by my side at Long's Wharf till the mill exploded, and then we turned our efforts to cutting trees for the Crown. I hadn't kept up with Cotton after Paul and I were jailed for holding back some of the best white pine for the colony's use.

"You always had a knack for working with your hands. Making rope and rigging sounds like a natural fit for you."

Cotton inspected his hands, turning them over several times. He pointed to several new callouses on the palms. "Natural? Don't know about that. See these? Started out as rope burns. And these?" He pointed to the tips of his fingers. "Never had callouses on my fingers before!"

He laughed, and I joined in, glad to have my old friend back. But it was time to be serious.

"We've not seen you at the Green Dragon for a while. We could use your help. A few of us are thinking about taking back some of the goods that Paxton and his customs agents have confiscated. Won't you join us?"

"You mean stealing? No, I don't think that's such a good idea. I still remember the last time you asked me to help. Didn't turn out so good for me. Your sister abandoned me, and I ended up in jail!"

Immediately, he mentions Molly's rejection.

"I wish I could tell you it will be different. Probably will be. Could be. Come on, Cotton, you know it will be. Molly's moved on. You should too."

Cotton and I were the same height, and now he looked me straight in the eye.

"Sure, why not. It's not like I have anything to lose."

For a split instant, his eyes narrowed. I wasn't sure I saw it. I chose to ignore it.

While the women of Boston steeped dried herbs and ground burnt peas to pass as tea, we men tended to more pressing political issues. To give all citizens a voice in Boston's affairs, Sam Adams, John Hancock, James Otis, and the rest of the Assembly formed the Body of the People. For the first time in its history, Boston would be ruled by all its people, not just the upper sort. The Body will determine how we respond to the Townshend Acts. Last week, more than half of Boston packed the South Meeting House. Tonight's numbers may surpass that.

Adams stepped up on the dais to alert the Body to Governor Bernard's request for troops.

"Our esteemed Governor," he coughed, "at the request of Lieutenant Governor... "

"Ssssssss! Ssssssss!" The people jeered at hearing mention of the colony's highest-ranking officials, Francis Bernard and Thomas Hutchinson.

"Quiet!" James Otis bellowed as he struggled to his feet in the front row. "Let the man speak. Rein in your feelings until he has finished!" When the crowd quieted, Otis nodded at Adams to begin once more.

"As I said, Lt. Governor Hutchinson has urged the governor to request additional troops be sent to Boston to keep the peace."

"Soldiers? Keep the peace?" A loud voice in the back called out. "It's them that's disturbing the peace!"

The Body roared in unison and stomped their feet in approval.

"Order! Order!" Otis pounded his cane for emphasis.

Molineux and I exchanged looks. This meeting could end in pandemonium if Otis didn't gain control. Molineux nodded, and we stood and made our way to opposite sides of the large room—ready to serve as sergeants-at-arms if needed.

Adams motioned with his arms and, shouting to be heard above the din, appealed for calm amidst the boos and catcalls.

"'Tis better to be informed than caught by surprise," he said. "Governor Bernard sent a query to General Gage in Halifax. We don't know the situation in Canada. It could be that Gage has no troops to spare and we're worrying needlessly. However, until we're certain that the general won't send troops, we'd be wise to prepare ourselves for an influx of Regulars."

"And what would you have us do?" shouted a voice from the back.

"If you are men, behave like men; let us take up arms immediately and be free and seize all the King's officers!"[4]

Those words had barely left his mouth when the Body of the People stood to cheer. For all the backslapping and huzzahs, I wondered whether everyone in the building owned the winning lottery ticket.

The Body's response concerned me. I hadn't anticipated a call to arms, but those in attendance were more than willing to heed Sam's invitation to violence. Molineux and I could urge the Sons of Liberty to keep the peace for a time, but if Adams's words kept watering the seeds of insurrection, our efforts wouldn't result in a lasting truce.

♥

The following day, Benjamin Edes stopped by the tavern to bend his elbow as well as my ear.

"I thought I recognized your voice last night," I said by way of greeting.

Edes sheepishly smiled and winked.

"Couldn't resist egging on ole Sam."

"Did you get the response you sought?"

He tossed the morning's newspaper on the bar and grinned widely. "Yes, I did!"

SEPTEMBER 28, 1768

Molly Weston

"What's all the fuss?" I peeked out of Anna's shop windows to watch the passersby. "Everyone's heading to the harbor."

"Do you think they've finally arrived? The troops?" Anna regarded the stacked gloves she'd fitted into a wall niche, dark leather at the bottom and cream on top, and adjusted them for easy access.

"Who knows? But all this commotion would indicate... " my voice trailed off.

Without raising her eyes, she said, "Why don't you go and see what has everyone's attention. Obviously, whatever is happening outside is more interesting than shopping in here. If it is the British, best to know sooner than later."

I grabbed my shawl and knotted it over my shoulders as I joined the stream of pedestrians heading south on Fish Street. Within two blocks, the massing crowd grew so thick we couldn't move forward. I stood on my toes and craned my neck to see above or between the heads. Those who could already see groaned. Placing my hands on the shoulders of the man in front of me, I stretched a bit more until a shift in the crowd opened a line of sight. To my left, and far in the distance, the towering masts of five British ships reached skyward on the Atlantic.

I sucked in my breath at the vision—the invasion. To my right lay the Three Lions, and I threaded my way to the tavern. Anna would find out soon enough about the soldiers' arrival.

A tumultuous scene greeted me. Father and Paul ferried trays of ale to the tables. Agitated drinkers packed in, shoulder to shoulder, each trying to speak over the others. The resulting cacophony of shouting men drove me into the kitchen to escape.

"Mother! Have you seen? Yes, of course you have," I babbled.

"It was bound to happen once Governor Bernard made the request."

"I counted five ships. Did Gage have to send so many soldiers?"

Eli burst through the back door. "Where's Geoffrey?"

Mother and I jumped at the sudden intrusion and looked at him as if he were daft.

"On patrol? At the Customs House?" I incredulously offered my brother the only two possibilities where Geoffrey spent his days.

"No. I'm hoping he knows more about these ships. Dr. Warren received word that more are on their way to Boston."

Mother and I exchanged glances at this news.

"Where did you hear that?" I didn't want to believe that even more soldiers would be disembarking in my city.

Eli ignored my question. "You've not seen him? Paul... " He muttered to himself and entered the great room.

Mother busied herself at the cupboard. "Now that you're home early, let's get supper started. All these mouths will want to be fed."

I sighed and tied an apron at my waist. Tension gathered in my shoulders, and my head ached. Food in those jabbering mouths would deaden the noise.

Eli Weston

I found Father filling tankards of ale while Paul skirted tables picking up the emptied ones.

"Good. We can use your help. Take these over there," Father pointed to a table near the door.

Although I wasn't at the tavern to serve, I couldn't disobey him, at least not with a roomful of customers. It was at times like these that we needed Henry the most.

I deposited the tankards and collected a few empties on my way back to the bar. Paul joined me in carrying them into the kitchen for a quick wash.

"No, Geoffrey's not been around today, not even for lunch," Paul responded to my query.

♥

Geoffrey appeared at the tavern after supper had been served and cleared. He nodded at me from across the room that still held a nearly full complement of drinkers and storytellers. A few men looked up from their tables when the flash of red appeared, but recognizing the familiar soldier's face, they turned back to their discussions. Nevertheless, Geoffrey strode towards the kitchen rather than eating amongst hot-tempered drunks and risking a confrontation.

It wasn't until late in the evening that business slowed enough for me to carry two mugs of ale into the kitchen.

"Doesn't look good," I said.

"No, in fact, it couldn't look bleaker. Bridgewater ordered the Quartering Act to be strictly enforced. As of tomorrow, we will be scouting locations suitable for billeting two regiments."

"What was Gage thinking, sending that many troops? Where does he think they'll be quartered? We've barely enough space for the regiment already here."

Geoffrey looked disgusted. "That's of no concern to General Bridgewater. He'll throw a family out of their house if necessary."

♥

It was nearly midnight before I closed the kitchen door and made my way down Gallups Alley toward the *Gazette* office. Benjamin needed to know about Bridgewater's orders.

Ben opened the door before I could knock. He ushered me into the back of the printing shop, where he struck a match to light a second lamp. The flame flickered high and then dropped low as he adjusted the wick.

"You've already heard then?" I asked.

"Hasn't everybody seen the ships?"

"Two regiments... four thousand men. Today's ships are only the beginning of what we'll need to prepare for."

Ben jumped to his feet at hearing the number of soldiers about to disembark. "Four thousand! That's not a peace-keeping force; that's an invasion! What with one regiment already here," he paused as if thinking, "that's nearly a third of the city's population. People won't be happy about quartering that many *Englanders*."

"Bernard and Hutchinson got their wish—protection from their own people."

"Ha!" Ben laughed half-heartedly. "Protection? That's one way to look at the numbers. As for me, this is another poke on the head. How do you import this many soldiers and tell people their presence is to enforce British laws? This large number isn't enforcement, it's coercion."

He started pacing and thinking aloud. "The soldiers will disembark soon... *Gazette* publishes Monday... too late... but maybe we can get the Sons to spread the word."

"I'll talk to Molineux in the morning. He can help. How much damage do we want to do?"

♥

I found William at his warehouse the next morning as he sorted door fixtures. There, I related my conversation with Benjamin Edes.

"Shouldn't be too difficult to arrange some sort of protest, Eli. Just depends on the severity of the message we want to send to General Gage and Britain. The South Enders are restless and ready to inflict some pain."

"Such as?"

"Merchant row on Long Wharf has lots of second-story windows perfect for a shot. We can line up shooters, wait till these uninvited guests are lined up beneath."

"Whoa! That's a bit drastic, William. Eventually, the soldiers'll fire back. Keep in mind, there'll be thousands of them against what? Maybe twenty shooters?"

"It'd be bloody, for sure. But then they'd understand that we don't want soldiers here."

"Still, we don't want to initiate any bloodshed. Perhaps a calmer approach?"

The merchant looked down, shook his head, and smiled at my reticence for violence. He raised his eyes to meet mine. "Then a calm riot it shall be."

September 29, 1768

Eli Weston

"Bernard insists that these new troops are here to enforce British laws. Nothing else." Dr. Warren drained his mug. It clanged as he slammed it on the table.

A few Sons of Liberty had gathered at the Green Dragon to discuss the newly arrived regiments.

"Such foolishness!" Sam Adams paced the second-floor meeting room. "Of course, he knows what the British are doing here. He's an addle-pated gollumpus who's forsaken his fellow citizens. He's been in the government's purse for so long that his allegiance is solely to the Crown."

"Master over the serfs in his kingdom?" Molineux interrupted.

His comment caught me in mid-gulp, and I sprayed my ale over the table. Molineux dabbed at his coat and glared at me. I coughed up the final drops in my throat before speaking.

"What makes sense is some civil disobedience."

"You've finally come 'round to my way of business!" shouted Molineux.

I ignored the good-natured taunt. "What we can do, gentlemen, is ignore the Quartering Act."

"Bernard's acquired four thousand deputies to see that the law's carried out, and your suggestion is to break it," the doctor warned.

"What would you have us do?"

"I'll hear you out."

"Boston's already quartered a thousand soldiers. We'd have to open up our barns and warehouses." I scanned the room and pointed at various individuals. "Do you want to invite soldiers to live in your houses, occupy your bedrooms, eat in your kitchen, always feeling that you're being watched? You know that The Three Lions houses four—we're full up—and the few empty houses available to let in the city won't accommodate the new arrivals. If all the merchants agree, we *can* limit where the soldiers live."

"What are you really saying?" Adams stopped pacing to face me.

"Let's get the upper hand. Force the soldiers to quarter in one or two areas rather than spread throughout the city. Corral them like we do livestock."

Molineux slapped the table with an open hand. "That's it! All the better to keep watch over their activities. But where?"

"The hall would be Bernard's choice," Adams said in a low voice.

"Faneuil Hall?" I asked, but knew before he nodded that the hall would be the governor's best option.

"Better there than in our homes," I replied. "Even so, the hall won't hold all of them."

"Treat 'em like the cattle they are. Let them have the Common!" Edes shouted. "They won't last the winter in tents!"

The men stomped their approval. Once the room quieted, Adams began drafting a letter to Governor Bernard outlining our demands.

OCTOBER 1, 1768

MOLLY WESTON

"But I want to go."

"There will be too many people. It will be chaotic," Paul warned. "You heard Eli—Molineux's thinking of shooting at the soldiers as they march through town. If that happens... " He shook his head.

"Then I'll be there to help the wounded."

He turned to Mother. "Will you please tell her to stay put? It won't be a good day to be in public."

"I think that she's proved her mettle. She should go. It's a parade, after all, not a riot."

I grinned at my brother in triumph.

Paul whistled lowly and shrugged in resignation. "Then I'll accompany you." He pointed a finger at me. "And don't you even think of leaving my side!"

Since September 28, when we spotted the first ships, more had sailed into the harbor. The ships anchored offshore, awaiting their turn to dock at the end of Long Wharf and discharge the human cargo. Paul and I found a good vantage point midway down the wharf, which gave us a panoramic view of the harbor and all the sailing vessels it held.

Several of the larger ships lowered dinghies filled with soldiers who rowed to the end of the pier. There they waited their turn, bobbing atop the waves like red algae, while lobsters from other watercraft disembarked.

One by one, each soldier climbed up a rickety wooden ladder and stepped to the far side of the pier's end. As their numbers grew on land, the men organized themselves into rows and columns. Eight abreast, those on land marched toward the city while others continued to disembark. Upon passing the single-story buildings that comprised Merchant's Row, Long Wharf became King Street, and there a band of American soldiers greeted the British. They performed a quick about-face, and the entire entourage then stepped in unison.

I tugged at Paul's sleeve. "Come on! We'll see more in town than here."

We retreated from the pier and, on the sidewalk, paralleled the soldiers as they marched toward the city. The two of us, however, moved more quickly than the men encumbered by heavy packs and a 10-pound firearm. We passed throngs of people lining both sides of King Street and continued westward. The State House, as well as other government buildings, displayed flags and banners that brightened their ochre exteriors. It was closer to the State House, where we found our new viewing position.

Pockets of loyalists dotted the sidewalks, filled four-person deep. They turned out wearing colorful finery for today's spectacle: men in their finest linen coats of blue and brown, women in imported silks and brocades in yellow, pink, and red. Fans of feather and lace refreshed the ladies from the heat of Indian summer. My brown petticoat paled in beauty. A high-pitched shriek drew my attention away from the fashions. A young boy excitedly chased another up and down the street, a game of tag in full cry.

The unlikely harmony of tinkling fifes and the resonant rat-a-tat-tat of drums beating cadence reached our ears. And so, the fanfare began.

Following the rows of American soldiers, the British proudly trooped their flag. The red, white, and blue of the Union Jack snapped in the brisk wind. Next up were the fifers and the drummers. The musicians, children really, played and rapped their instruments without missing a note. It was difficult not to tap my foot to the tune, even knowing that this light-hearted music foreshadowed trouble for my city. Finally came the soldiers; row after row of red-coated soldiers filed down the roadway.

Paul and I stood sandwiched between two loyalist families. The men clapped loudly and cheered as the soldiers passed; their wives smiled, occasionally nodded, and tapped their fans on gloved hands. I itched to find company more in agreement with my views.

After watching a few rows of stony-faced redcoats demonstrate their marching prowess, Paul poked me in the ribs and whispered, "Watch this."

"Hey, you, blunderbuss! Get back on the ship that dropped you!" he shouted at the nearest soldier.

I shot him an incredulous look, as did the fellow on my right.

"Bloody scrubs! Couldn't find any work on your side of the ocean?"

"Watch your mouth, you uneducated cur!" The fellow chided Paul. His wife forgot her upbringing and chastised my brother as well. "Such riffraff!"

The blue-coated gentleman grasped his wife's elbow and led her away. "Let's remove ourselves from this lowlife."

Others up and down King Street followed Paul's lead, jeering as the soldiers progressed on their meandering route to Faneuil Hall. A few soldiers scowled at the hecklers, but no one broke ranks.

I sighed. It wasn't enough that we were losing one of our meeting places and markets, but of all things, we were losing it to an occupying army.

"How many has it been?" I finally asked Paul.

"Not even close to the four thousand who'll have to disembark. Had enough of this pageantry yet?"

I could barely hear him over the loyalist huzzahs and clapping. Leaning in, I asked, "Say again?"

Before Paul could repeat his question, from behind me, I heard a man speak, "Why are you standing there and watching? I wouldn't even look at them."

A woman's reply made me smile. "Ha! You're a pretty fellow! You said that you would fight up to your knees in blood to destroy them, and now you won't even look at them!"[5]

Paul caught my eye and smirked. "Let's be off."

The Town of Boston in New England and British Ships of War Landing Their Troops 1768. Engraving by Paul Revere. From the Library of Congress.

November 1768

HESTER WINSLOW

"Oh, I do not like this!"

"What's that? You're muttering again." Cyrus stood behind me, closing the clasp on my strand of pearls.

"Nothing important." I turned and planted a kiss on his cheek. I fondled the pearls, admiring the smooth coolness of the round jewels that weighed against my bosom, a recent gift from my Cyrus. "These are lovely! Thank you, dear husband."

Cyrus caressed my face and returned the kiss. "Are you sure you don't want me to accompany you this evening?"

"A sweet gesture, but I'll be fine. It will be a dull evening for you as we women chat about our activities."

"I worry about the assaults on women. The soldiers are more brazen every day. Let me get the carriage."

"Pshaw! I'd prefer to walk. Besides, those soldiers wouldn't dare attempt anything against a loyalist. They are our protectors, after all. Stop worrying. You're sounding like a nursemaid, and I'm too old for one."

With that, I donned my navy mantua and picked up a cream lace-trimmed cap. It would have been nice to have the carriage, but I couldn't risk Cyrus learning where I was going. After a quick glimpse in the mirror, I headed into the dusky evening. Clouds dappled the moon, filtering its light and darkening the streets. The lamplighter hadn't yet passed by the first block, which made the streets all the blacker. I walked quickly to keep my nerves at bay.

Although I couldn't admit it to my husband, I was nervous, but not because of the aggressions against women. Soldiers were attacking women of the lower sort—the ones who frequented taverns and the wharves at night. That didn't apply to me. No, my anxiety was due to an unexpected meeting. For the first time, General Bridgewater sent word calling for an evening appointment. He wanted information I still hadn't acquired. That blasted Cotton! My heart fluttered from nerves, and I pushed away the desperation roiling in my belly.

I had to walk only eight blocks; surely, I'd think of something to satisfy my employer.

I turned the corner onto Sudbury Street and then walked along Mount Street till it became Common. My nerves jangled, and I heard my heart beat louder the closer I drew to Boston Common. It was one thing to watch the soldiers drilling in daylight, yet passing by their encampment at night made me shudder. Dusk opened the door to all sorts of nefarious behavior.

Raucous voices down the street roused me from my thoughts. I peered ahead searching for clues to identify the men, but it wasn't until they passed under a streetlamp that I could see they were soldiers. My core stiffened, and my heartbeat deadened all other sounds. I glanced to the left, thinking to cross the street, but I was too late.

"Hey, boys, look at this. A pretty lady all by herself." The leader of the pack sauntered toward me, his eyes studying me top to bottom.

Involuntarily, I stepped backward.

"Oh, no, you don't!" A second soldier appeared at my side, too close to be respectful.

I swallowed and prayed my voice would be steady.

"Gentlemen, please move aside. I have an appointment." I veered to the right and stepped forward.

The leader matched my pace. "An appointment? At this time of night?" He laughed, and the others conformed to his example.

Their vicious snickering unsettled me, and I feared what they might do. "Again, I ask you to step aside. My appointment is with General Bridgewater. He'll not be happy with you if I'm late."

The men roared at the mention of the general's name. The leader doubled over and slapped his thighs in glee. He raised his head, looked me in the eye, and then laughed harder.

Wanting to take advantage of his incapacity, once more, I stepped forward.

His laughter stopped suddenly, and he seized my arm. "You won't be meeting the general. At least not yet."

I shrieked as he grabbed me and jerked my arm down as I turned inward and ducked under his arm. The quick movement surprised him, and I ran across the street.

"Help me! Help me!"

The door to Edes & Gill Printing opened, and Eli Weston and Benjamin Edes ran out to see the commotion. I flew into Ben's arms, and Eli headed for the soldiers.

"Get away from here! Leave our women alone!" he yelled.

Ben put his arm around my waist and escorted me into the shop. He sat me down and squatted in front of me.

"Are you all right?"

"Yes, no, I'm not sure. They gave me a good fright."

"What are you doing out by yourself? You know these soldiers are on the prowl."

"I thought I'd be fine."

Eli entered the shop and pulled up a chair. "They're heading toward the wharf. You won't see them again." He leaned in. "Just where are you going after dark?"

"I asked her the same question." Ben turned toward me. "It's time you told us what you're doing. No lady, and I repeat, *lady*, would be out by herself after dark these days."

Eli poked Ben in the ribs. "It does look suspicious, doesn't it?"

GEOFFREY CANFIELD

Eli caught up with me near Faneuil Hall; I was heading toward The Three Lions, having finished patrol duty, and he was heading home after working a full day at Long Wharf. He lost no time in telling me about being with Ben Edes at the *Gazette* offices when they saved Hester from some roving regulars.

I am ashamed of my fellow soldiers. Unbridled, reckless behavior—wanton behavior—toward American women almost daily. I cannot abide these acts, but the general is slow to punish the perpetrators. Bridgewater is always searching for a way to bedevil the Americans, and I can't help but think he is manipulating this misconduct as a means to incite them.

"I hate to think of what might have happened had you and Ben not heard her cries," I said.

"They didn't seem worried at her mention of General Bridgewater. Apparently, she believed that mentioning his name would send them running. Instead, it merely spurred them to action."

"Yes, I've often thought that the general is lax about enforcing lapses in conduct. I know we've both cautioned Molly and Elizabeth about being out after dark."

"However, it did give me and Ben a chance to question Hester about the general, especially about being out late on her way to meet with him."

His comment put me on alert. Nothing good ever came from a meeting with Bridgewater. "What did she say?"

"Ben pushed her, but all she would admit to was having an assignation with him. I suppose she thought she could pass it off as a tryst." Eli laughed.

The thought of a young, beautiful American woman carrying on with the older, ugly, and fat general made me chuckle. Soon, I joined Eli in laughter.

"She really does think everyone else is lacking intelligence, doesn't she?"

Molly Weston

"We'll have to make do." Mother scraped the bottom of the crock for the last of the beans and added them to the kettle of boiling water.

"I'll get the rest of the bacon."

"No, let's save that. I'd rather your father and brothers get what little meat we have than the customers."

"I'll make an extra loaf of rye bread to fill their stomachs, and they can have a bean supper. But, you know, I could ask Geoffrey for some money."

Mother looked up sharply. "What?"

"Just a bit to tide us over. It's costing us to feed these soldiers. Look at our larder! It's practically empty. I'm sure he wouldn't mind."

"It grieves your father and me to be in this position. We never thought we'd be feeding and housing these soldiers for so long. It's been nearly four years now," Mother complained.

"That's why I want to ask. It's only fair that they contribute. The Crown expects us to pay for their soldiers who shouldn't even be here. This situation is so frustrating!" I slammed the sack of flour on the table so hard that clouds of swirling powder rose above my head.

"Well, don't scatter what we can't afford to waste!" Mother teased good-naturedly.

I winked at her. "I'm going to ask Geoffrey tomorrow. He can't refuse."

Eli came downstairs for breakfast as Mother and I finished our conversation.

As I poured him a cup of coffee, he said, "You'll never guess who we ran into last night. And I do mean *ran into*."

"Why don't you tell us, son, or we'll be guessing till suppertime."

"Hester Winslow."

I nearly dropped the bowl of porridge in front of him. I hadn't expected to hear that name. "Who? Stop teasing."

"Ben and I were talking business when we heard a woman screaming. No sooner had we stepped out of the shop than Hester ran into us. Ben took her inside."

"What was she doing?"

"At that moment, she was running from some soldiers. Which, by the way, is why I don't like you going about at night."

I didn't respond to his pointed remark, instead focusing on Hester's actions. "I mean, what was she doing out by herself? And by the Common? That seems so odd. I'd think that even she wouldn't dare walk by so many bachelors after sunset. She's such a social creature—nearly every night she and Cyrus have some sort of engagement."

"That's why it seemed so peculiar to us that she was alone," Eli continued. "After calming down, she admitted to having an appointment with General Bridgewater."

"Oh, no! She was questioning me again a couple of weeks ago about the scars on my wrists."

Eli raised his eyebrows at my admission, but remained mute.

"I didn't tell her anything about the black powder."

My brother tapped his spoon against the bowl. "How did you explain the scars without mentioning the powder?"

"I just kept making up stories. I'm sure she didn't believe me."

Eli looked pensive. Maybe it's time you told her about Jack and Salmon abducting you, but nothing else. It would feed her insatiable curiosity for a bit, just don't tell her when it happened or where."

"I could do that. She was obviously meddling; nobody asks that many questions without having a surreptitious scheme." I thought back to my conversation with Hester that afternoon at the coffee house. "It was curious; she kept leaning in and looking so interested. She's never shown such concern for me." I reached for Eli's cup to refill it.

"She's always been a busybody," Mother grumbled.

"Between us, I think we have a solution for her prying behavior."

"What are you planning, Eli?"

December 1768

Eli Weston

"Well, hello, Christopher. How'd your lessons go?" I continued to tally the tavern's monthly expenses and barely glanced at the young fellow as he approached.

"Do I have to go tomorrow? I'd rather stay here with Paul and play with Boots."

"Of course, you have to go. That's part of our agreement for you working at The Three Lions."

"I can learn when I'm not in school."

"Oh, really?" I turned to face the lad. "And what sort of lesson do you master on your own, or do you have an instructor outside of the schoolroom?"

"I know things, things that would surprise you."

I chuckled at Christopher's earnestness. "Let me judge how well you learned your lesson then."

The boy puffed up his chest and looked me straight in the eye. "I know that you blew up the old grist mill."

I ended the lighthearted banter by gripping his arms tightly. "Where did you hear that?"

"Ouch! Let go!"

"Sorry, Christopher. This is important. Where did you hear about the mill? Who told you?"

"You'll be angry with me."

"I won't. I promise. But it really is important that you be honest with me right now."

"On my way home from school, I sometimes pass by the Common. I like to watch the soldiers practicing."

"The Common isn't anywhere near Mrs. Althorp's, the tavern, or the school for that matter."

Christopher's eyes shone with defiance, as much as a ten-year-old dares to oppose his elders.

"If I walk through the Common, it takes longer to get home. Sometimes I'd rather be walking than at Missus Althorp's. Now that I work here, I don't go by there much anymore."

I remembered the lad's wretched homelife and couldn't fault his need to be out from under that atmosphere.

"So, what did you learn? How to load and fire a rifle?" I pressed him again, hoping his lesson wasn't as laden with as much accurate information as I feared.

"If I had a rifle, I bet I could load it. Maybe even shoot it!" Christopher raised his imaginary firearm and pointed it at Boots lying by the hearth.

"Whoa! What about the other things you saw? And you said you heard something."

The boy positioned his rifle at his side before answering. "Like I said, I was at the Common and saw Mister Cotton and Missus Hester. Arm in arm, like they was good friends."

I whistled lowly. I didn't want to let Chris in on all the details yet. It wouldn't be good for a talkative boy to inadvertently say something that wouldn't bode well for Geoffrey and me.

"I know Missus Hester doesn't like Miss Molly much." He studied me somberly. "Miss Molly and Missus Elizabeth talk about her a lot. I don't think they like her. Sometimes they don't know I'm listening."

"Go on."

"They didn't see me, so I slowed down and followed them a bit. That's when I heard it."

"Did Cotton say anything else? Did either of them mention somebody else?"

Christopher's cheeks pinked a bit. "Well, they did say something about a bridge and Lieutenant Canfield. And somethin' about you, too."

"Ah," I leaned back and looked at the ceiling. Our young charge was indeed craftier than we believed.

"Chris, it seems you do learn things outside of school. Let's keep this bit quiet. We don't want Molly or Mrs. Elizabeth to hear that you're out walking the streets."

"So, then you won't tell them?"

"No. Let's shake on it."

Chris pumped my hand with more strength than I could have imagined, and then he winked. "Our secret."

I watched the little lad as he reported for afternoon tavern duty. Not sure how long I could rely on the young boy's promise of silence, I headed out to find Geoffrey.

Geoffrey Canfield

Eli found me on the wharf as I reviewed the *Princess of India*'s bill of lading. I winced seeing the entry for tea, knowing it was destined for a warehouse rather than a kettle, but my friend's first words made me boil.

"Your reservations about Bridgewater may be grounded in fact."

"You're saying that all the time I felt he knew something, he did?"

"No. There's too much we don't know to be sure of what he knew and when he found out, but this afternoon I learned he has reason to suspect you and me in the mill blast."

I exhaled and felt deflated in more than my lungs.

"Evidently, you know more than you've said."

"And I'll give you the details over dinner."

Eli left as abruptly as he appeared, leaving my head swimming with too many questions that had no answers. Is there a chance of repairing the damage to my reputation? If not, would I have time to sell my commission before being dismissed? Or in the worst case, would I be charged with treason?

If he were correct about Bridgewater, then my days as a member of the King's Royal Army were coming to an end. Molly and I needed to make our own arrangements if we were to have a future together.

Eli Weston

I aimed my feet toward the ropewalks and Cotton. If I were to believe Christopher's story, my friend and the thorn in my sister's life conspired together. His young ears may not understand the language of adults, especially ideas that are heavy with innuendo and double entendre. Entire words may escape his understanding. But no matter what the boy heard or understood, Cotton and I needed to sweep clean any misunderstandings between us.

"You had no right!" I pounded the table with my fist and glared at my supposedly best friend. "Not that long ago, Geoffrey and I asked for your help, which you wholeheartedly agreed to give."

"To your own detriment, Eli."

Cotton agreed to meet me in The Three Lions' kitchen after the dinner hour, but I quickly escorted him upstairs to my room, where Geoffrey awaited us.

"As you say, you came to me. I did not seek you out. Why would I? You turned your back on me. You chose your British friend over me."

"We grew up together, Cotton. Years of studying and working, side by side, bound us tighter than brothers. Truly, you cannot believe that making a new friend would cast you out of my life."

I had wanted to ask about his conversation with Hester, but he nimbly changed the topic to one nearer his heart.

"And yet, what reparations were given for spending time in jail? And your friend didn't actually free me; he foisted that task onto Matthew." He pounded his thumb into his chest. "In the end, it was me, ME, who found Molly and got her back to Boston. Not your chum."

Geoffrey broke into the two-way conversation.

"You've twisted everything. You've known Molly since she toddled about, but you never showed an ounce of anything other than brotherly affection until you discovered her interests lay with another."

"If you truly cared, you'd have found her sooner."

Cotton's mention of the fire at the mill irritated me; Geoffrey's eyes flared with anger. I planted a firm hand on Geoffrey's shoulder to keep him seated and turned to Cotton.

"You reject our friendship for a love that never was. But dismissing me also rejects Molly. She never harmed you."

Cotton narrowed his eyes and sneered. "Ah, yes. Molly. It always comes back to your sister, doesn't it? The lovely Molly can do no wrong."

"You betrayed Geoffrey because Molly loves him and not you?"

"Finally, the brother recognizes the truth."

"You never loved her, or you wouldn't speak ill of her." Geoffrey grabbed Cotton by the collar and dragged him across the table.

I pulled at Geoffrey's right arm till he loosened his grip. Cotton slumped down on the bench and rubbed his neck. He fell silent, but his eyes blazed with bitterness the fracas hadn't quenched.

Geoffrey straightened his jacket and huffed, splotched cheeks the only hint of anger. And then he paced.

I joined him in thought and matched his steps. Cotton's slitted eyes watched us, a smirk curled his lips. I could've smacked him.

Once my ire faded, I sat facing my friend. As I gazed at the man I'd known since childhood, sadness and a bit of emptiness consumed me, and I mourned the loss of such a long friendship.

Cotton finally broke the silence. "Did you think I'd put Molly in danger? You think me capable of that?"

"Didn't you?" Geoffrey spoke before I could answer. "Ever since Molly and I sealed our bond, you've worked against us."

"Why wouldn't I?" Cotton's upper lip rose in disgust. "You, with your rank, your pretty uniform, your father's money—you have all that, and still you pursue an American. You could have any girl in London."

"Enough! I won't hear any more from the two of you. Molly made her decision, and Father agreed with her choice. Any other idea of yours, Cotton, is wishful thinking."

Cotton and Geoffrey glowered at one another, but I ignored the intensity of their stares.

I steered the conversation away from talk of my sister. It was time to learn the depth of trouble we faced. "What's your relationship with Hester Winslow? What did you tell her?"

"And why?" Spittle flew from Geoffrey's mouth. "But then we know why, don't we? All to destroy me."

Cotton scratched his chin. "You aren't wrong."

Geoffrey lunged, right arm back and raised, ready to deliver a powerful jab to his adversary's temple. I flung my left arm into the blow's path and felt the impact jolt me to the bone, throwing me off balance. I stumbled and fell into the hearth tripod.

"Devil be damned!"

I spun around and glared at Geoffrey and Cotton. Pointing my finger at the two hotheads, I didn't hold back.

"Get this choler out now, both of you! Your anger serves no purpose other than inflaming the situation. We find ourselves, and I do mean all of us," I glared at Cotton to make the point, "in grave danger. Doesn't matter any longer who said what to whom. All three of us are responsible for the black powder and the mill."

Geoffrey perched on the edge of a bench, rested his forearms on his thighs, and clasped his hands together. "No matter our feelings for one another, our fates are intertwined." He looked at me and Cotton. "Do either of you see a way for us not to hang?"

January 1769

GEOFFREY CANFIELD

Eli, Molly, and Paul joined me in my sleeping quarters after dinner to discuss Hester's relationship with General Bridgewater. The walls grew closer as my friends brought in more chairs to fit into the empty spaces around the small dressing table and bed. A scratching noise and soft mew meant the last attendee had arrived—Buttermilk. While the cat perambulated our legs and those of the chairs, Eli sketched his plan on a slate.

"It's fairly simple. We know that Hester's been needling Cotton and Molly for information about the black powder. And Cotton's been doing a pretty good job at misleading her." Eli scribbled their names onto the board and drew a line from each to the name *Hester*.

Paul jumped into the discussion while Eli drew a line from *Hester* to a new name, *Bridgewater*. "If we provide the information to her, then we control what the general finds out. Or doesn't."

"Can we trust Cotton? I dislike raising the point, but you know our rapport is rather weak. Not to mention our previous disagreements." I spread my hands, shrugged my shoulders, and tried to look contrite.

Molly chuckled at my effort and reached down to rub Buttermilk's belly. "No need to be so apologetic, Geoffrey. Can't we agree that those days are long gone?"

Paul, on the other hand, guffawed. "That fistfight was one to remember. The way you hauled back to land your fist on his nose!"

I interrupted him. "That's enough. No need to recite all that happened."

Eli rapped on the table. "If you've finished discussing Cotton and Geoffrey's relationship, can we map out what information we want Hester to give to the general?"

Molly sighed in exasperation. "For all the time you've been tracking the tidesmen to find out how to get into the warehouses, why haven't you asked Cotton to feed Hester information about the tea?"

I, for one, couldn't believe that none of us had thought of that. We had focused solely on the wine crates, but of course, tea shipments had been confiscated as well.

She continued. "Several times, she's whisked me out of Anna's shop to have coffee, but we always end up at the coffeehouses where the proprietors serve tea, if you know how to ask for it."

We all jumped at hearing a thump outside the door. I raced to open it, ready to attack whoever was eavesdropping.

To our surprise, Christopher was rubbing his elbow and grinning up at me.

HESTER WINSLOW

"Missus Winslow! Someone at the door for you," our maid, Bessie, called up the staircase.

"In a moment." I adjusted the ribbons on my mauve stomacher and tucked a few ash blonde curls under my cap. As I descended, I saw that dirty street urchin I'd seen at Boston Common. The creature began jabbering as soon as he saw me on the stairs.

"Missus Winslow! I got sumpin' for you. Here!" He thrust a folded paper towards me, even though I wasn't close enough to grasp it. I gazed at the young fellow as he stood, rooted in one spot and arm raised as if frozen, face beaming and waiting for me to draw near.

"Who sends you?" I plucked the paper from his hand.

His smile fled at my sharp tone. He dropped his head and began scuffing his boot on the Persian rug. "Mister Cotton, ma'am."

"Stop that! You'll dig a hole in the carpet."

"Yes, ma'am." The boy shrank even further.

I turned my back, opening the paper to read. I glanced behind me. The child remained. "What are you waiting for? A tip? You won't get one from me."

"No, ma'am," the tiny voice piped. "The mister said you'd want to send back a reply."

> *Hester,*
>   *Meet me tomorrow morning. 9 o'clock. Trinity Church.*
> *Same bench.*
>
>   *Cotton*

"Yes, I do have a reply for Mister Easton. Yes."

"What is it?"

"Yes!"

"Oh! You want me to tell him yes? I'll do that right away."

The door slammed before I could answer. From the front window, I watched the boy bound along Garden Street, an occasional skip and hop adorning his stride. His antics charmed me, and I laughed to myself.

♥

I wasn't so amused the next morning as I waited for Cotton to arrive. He had a lot of nerve to summon me and not show up at the appointed time. When we last met, he reneged on our deal. I retied my purse strings and played with different-sized bows as my agitation grew. Nothing occurred to me as a plausible reason for his desire to meet today. *So why am I here?*

"Good morning!"

The voice in my ear startled me. I leapt to my feet, my head colliding with his chin.

"Ouch!"

"My goodness! Why did you do that?" I felt the crown of my head, searching for the tender spot and possible swelling.

Cotton rubbed his chin and moved his jaw back and forth. "Still works."

The stinging pain eased a bit, but the impact soured my disposition. "Get it out in the open. Why did you want to meet?"

"I've been thinking about your offer. You see, what worked for you didn't work in my favor. No, don't say a word. You know it didn't. Since then, I've been pondering the situation."

I crossed my arms and studied the tall blond. "And your counteroffer is what?"

"The sticking point has always been telling the general about my involvement. That gives him enough wood to build my gibbet as well as that of the others. Needless to speak, I wasn't eager to supply the lumber."

"I told you that he wouldn't have pursued you had you come forward."

"Says you. I had no offer from the man himself."

I rubbed my temples and groaned in frustration. "Cotton, why are we here?"

"You need specific information to give the general. I'm not willing to do that."

"You're talking in circles, Cotton. I'm leaving." I rose from the bench, but he laid hold of the back of my mantua.

"Wait! I'm not done!" He gently tugged at my warm outer garment till I stepped back and sat down. He joined me on the bench, sitting sideways to face me.

My eyes bored into his; I wanted him to understand the degree of irritation I felt. "Then hurry up. The cold is seeping through to my toes."

"Ask General Bridgewater about Jack and Salmon. They are the ones who abducted Molly."

"I already know that. Molly told me."

"Ah! But she may not have relayed to you their involvement in the black powder explosion at the mill."

I tapped my foot. "You are exhausting my patience."

"Those two worked for the general."

My head snapped up. "What are you saying? The general hired them to kidnap Molly? Why would he do that?"

"But that's not all he's done. You see, Goody Winslow, General Bridgewater isn't the noble and righteous individual you deem him to be."

"Pshaw! I can't believe he would sanction such a deed, or anything else that you speak of. No, I won't hear another word." I stood and faced him. "You may not like the British, but you can't malign an officer like this."

Geoffrey Canfield

"Ha!" I slapped the rough-hewn table and guffawed at hearing Cotton's story.

"She just left? Before you could give her the reason for Jack and Salmon?" Eli sounded incredulous. "Did you even get to mention that he was seizing merchants' goods?"

"I barely got a word in before she up and left. Huffed off to tell her husband, I s'pose. Or maybe the general himself." Cotton grinned so wide it made my own jawline hurt. I gave it an empathetic rub. "But no, I didn't get a word out about the seizures."

Eli and I were conversing over tankards of ale when Cotton had burst through the tavern door. The three of us adjourned to the kitchen, where Paul joined us, carrying a sizeable mug for the new arrival.

"When will you see her again?" Eli asked Cotton. "Without the rest of the information, who knows what she'll concoct in that wee brain."

Eli was sincere, but the rest of us laughed at the image of that prideful woman with a shrunken head. Even Eli joined in, but after a moment of lightheartedness, he addressed his friend. "Seriously, Cotton, you must meet with her again."

"I shall. Where's that little go-between of yours?" Cotton stretched his neck and swiveled his head to examine every corner of the kitchen.

"You need me?" Christopher poked his head around the corner, from where he'd obviously been eavesdropping again.

"Yes, you. We have some work for you to do."

The young tavern worker glowed at the possibility of helping the adults. "I'm free now, or tomorrow, or whenever you need me," he said.

Cotton turned to face the rest of us. "That's commitment!"

Hester Winslow

Cotton's outrageous accusation against the general infuriated me. I walked briskly into the wind and soon found myself heading toward the wharf. Although I hadn't wanted to pass by so many soldiers and loiterers who frequented the seaside, neither did I want to go east toward the Common and risk running into the same soldiers who had frightened me two nights ago.

My eyes teared at the touch of the icy breeze, forcing me to walk with my head down so I could see the path. From time to time, a gust would blow me a step or two sideways. I gripped my mantua tightly and prayed my feet wouldn't slip on the ice before I reached my destination.

The British Coffee House signage appeared, and with a grateful heart, I entered the establishment. With a lacy handkerchief, I dabbed the corners of my eyes and searched for an empty table amidst the busyness. A handsome and well-dressed gentleman noticed me standing inside the door. He stood and beckoned me to join him. As there was no other place for me, I crossed the room.

"Let me take your wrap," he suggested. "The weather is acting rather cross, don't you think? Sit near the fire."

"You are very kind. The wind has taken every bit of warmth from me." I gazed at the man's face, taking in the green eyes topped by dark eyebrows and framed by a square jaw. A niggling thought occurred, but it flew away before landing.

"Commissioner William Burch, madam, at your service." He nodded his head as if he were meeting me on foot and bowing.

"Mrs. Cyrus Winslow. Thank you for sharing your table."

The commissioner ordered tea and sweet cakes for two from the server, reminding me of how much I adored a man taking charge. A sigh of contentment escaped my lips, and I folded my hands on the table.

"The tea will be lovely. Again, I must thank you." A coquettish lilt accented my words.

He smiled and winked. "I am the one to be thankful," he paused, "for a beautiful woman to spend her afternoon with me."

His words and flirtatious tone made me blush. "What brings you to this coffee house?"

"General Bridgewater. He speaks highly of this place, as well as of you." He reached out and gently patted my hand.

I gasped, now remembering where I had seen this man before. Here, at the British Coffee House, always in the background when the general and I met. Although the fire was near, my heart chilled, and I shivered involuntarily.

♥

"Oh, Missus Winslow, hurry and sit by the fire. You are chilled to the bone."

Bessie didn't realize how accurate her assessment was. I let her fuss over me, raising my feet onto a stool and tucking a woolen blanket around my shoulders and another under my legs.

"I'll bring some tea. Can I get you something to eat? A biscuit with butter and honey, perhaps?"

"Tea will suffice, Bessie. Is Mr. Winslow home?"

"Not yet, ma'am."

She bustled off to the kitchen, leaving me alone to reflect. All afternoon, I parried questions from Commissioner Burch, and now, when I wanted nothing more than to simply sit and thaw, troubling thoughts dripped through my mind faster than icicles melting on a spring day.

February 1769

Geoffrey Canfield

Bridgewater knows about the mill. About Eli and me. About us blowing up his cache of black powder. Because of us, the general's small fortune and quest for power in the colony disappeared in one big explosion. Governor Bernard is still trying to prosecute the Stamp Act rioters. It would be just like Bridgewater to do the same. What if he finds out about us trying to deplete his hoard of confiscated goods?

Thoughts plagued me as I paced in my quarters. The punishment for treason is harsh, and I quivered thinking of my parents' shame. The son of the Earl of Eastleigh, a traitor! I should be free to concentrate, yet the image of my body swinging from a noose and fellow soldiers quartering it while my heart still beat turned my insides to jelly.

Stiffen up! You knew what the road ahead could lead to. Keep your courage!

Buttermilk butted the door open and leaped onto the bed. She lay on her side and called to me in her gravelly voice. "Yeow."

I reached out to pet her flank, but she had other ideas. Instead, she pulled my hand to her face and began to nuzzle and lick me. My anxiety lessened as the tabby kissed and caressed my knuckles. Each time I withdrew my hand to stroke her, she forcibly grasped it with her paws and continued working her raspy tongue over my skin. I chuckled at her persistence in cleaning the same patch and wondered how long this show of affection could last.

Persistence is what Eli and I needed right now. If there were a way to sway Bridgewater's opinion of what he thinks, to convince him that his information was incorrect, it would happen because we continually present him with new deceptions. If we can keep the general distracted, we, and all of Boston, have a better chance at success.

♥

Eli was finishing supper when I sat across from him in a corner of the great room.

"Will we hang?" he asked before shoveling the last spoonful into his mouth.

"Not if I can help it." I turned toward the bar. "Paul, bring me an ale, and another for your brother."

"Mostly, it will depend on how well we can dismantle the fortress of information Cotton supplied to Hester."

"Well, the harridan is not known for her truthfulness, so that works in our favor," Eli added.

"Indeed. Additionally, we can use Jack and Salmon's abduction of Molly in our favor. I can't imagine that Bridgewater, as corrupt as he is, would ever condone such a move."

"Saying that our actions were simply to find my sister," he sighed. "Could it be enough?"

"Precisely what we need to ensure. Again, being quartered here at the tavern provides more than adequate reason for me to join you in the search."

Eli Weston

Cotton wasn't known for being schoolbook clever, and if I hadn't tutored him when we were younger, he'd still be in grammar school. But I'd always thought him smart in life skills, until he believed he could tell another of his part in the black powder explosion and escape punishment. I didn't want to think ill of my friend. Listening to him twist those events proved he didn't—or maybe couldn't—admit to being at fault. Perhaps it was the combination of a pretty face and the lure of promised rewards that convinced him he was invulnerable.

I moved through the city toward the ropewalk. Laborers jostled one another as they made their way to shops and businesses in the early morning. The sun burned off the seaside mist while the warming temperature awoke the stench of the tanners' vats of urine. Coopers whacked nails into barrel staves, the blows echoing through the alleyways. Merchants and shoppers filled the spaces in between as they verbally tussled over prices.

I looked down at the rag-wrapped sandwich I carried and released the tension in my hand. Too late. The lunch had a well-developed waist, even though it shouldn't have one. *Taste should be fine.* I shrugged and continued to Cotton's place of employment.

I found my friend at the far end of the shop. Cotton's hands continued to be his best asset. He excelled when we felled white pines in the forest, and now I watched him whipping the ends of a rope, finishing it properly. When he set it aside, he looked up and waved me over.

"Sorry. It got crushed." I handed him the sandwich.

"Wasn't expecting you to feed me," he replied, taking the sandwich. "You didn't make this, did you?"

I shook my head. "Since when have you known me to spend time in a kitchen if it weren't to eat? From Mother."

Cotton smiled, and it seemed as if my friend had returned— almost. I needed to tread carefully where he was concerned a while longer. *Let's see how he handles this first assignment.*

"This is what you need to tell Hester," I began.

♥

"Eli! Eli!"

A shrill voice called to me from the great room. Before I could answer his beck, Christopher ran into the kitchen. His cheeks flushed from exertion, and his skin glistened from heat and humidity. His eyes twinkled with excitement.

"Slow down!" I reached out to corral the youngster. "Let's not knock over the soup."

"He, he, he did it," Christopher panted.

"He? Who did what?"

Christopher's eyes popped wide in surprise.

"You don't know?"

I gazed at the tavern's youngest server and sat. I patted the space beside me on the bench, and Christopher plopped down.

"Could you speak in full sentences?"

"Cotton!" Christopher's shrill voice exclaimed. "You said he needed to tell that lady—"

"Young man, have you been listening at my door as well?"

Now Christopher's cheeks reddened from embarrassment. "It's the only way to know what's going on here. None of you ever tell me nuthin'."

I chuckled at his predicament.

"I suppose you didn't attend school today?"

"No, sir, I mean, yes, sir, I mean I did."

I arched an eyebrow.

"Honest. I, well, maybe I left early."

"How did you even know where they would be?"

Christopher puffed his chest with pride. "Cotton let me deliver a note to that lady's house. I read it, too."

♥

Later that night, Geoffrey laughed with me as I related Christopher's adventures.

"And that is how a spy is born," he added when I completed the tale. "Do you think he's mature enough to carry on with this messenger business?"

The question sobered me. A grown man may know what peril lies in subterfuge gone awry, yet a child may view the tasks as commonplace, totally unaware of danger lurking underneath.

"Certainly, he conducted himself adequately on Cotton's errand. Although," I added, "I'm not sure I would have entrusted him with such a missive. And to think he took it upon himself to read it before delivery."

Geoffrey nodded. "He's old enough to take pride in a job well done. So, perhaps he's competent too. In the end, we may be thankful the little imp has decided to work with us and not against."

MARCH 1769

ELI WESTON

I've recruited Paul, Warren, and Molineux to track Culmer and Senhouse. The tidesmen come ashore regularly to eat, drink, and plague our citizens. Tonight, I'll meet up with them at the Green Dragon.

♥

As I approached the Dragon, the door opened, and a sliver of light shone on the street, allowing me to recognize Culmer as he stepped out. I pulled my collar close to my face and silently stepped back into the shadow. Now that Providence had given me this opportunity, rather than meet up with the men, I chose to follow the tidesman from the opposite side of the street. In no hurry, he strolled toward Faneuil Hall and Merchants Row. *There's nothing for him down there. The merchant warehouses are empty.*

But as he passed the warehouses, it slowly dawned on me that, should he continue on this path, he would pass by the Stamp Master's house and then could end up at Oliver's Wharf. What better place to store confiscated goods than in the Stamp Master's own wharf? *But could it really be that easy?*

I kept pace with the tidesman long enough to ascertain that the wharf was his destination and then ran back to the Dragon with the good news.

APRIL 1769

Molly Weston

"Molly! Molly! Come quick!"

I chased after the high-pitched voice and found it in the kitchen. Christopher stood, wobbly arms extended, a trencher of steaming porridge in each hand. As the boy walked, the hot gray mush slopped over the sides.

"I can't hold it much longer!" he squealed when he saw me.

I raced over to relieve him of his burdens, and he collapsed onto a stool.

"Whatever are you doing?" I asked.

"Miss Elizabeth asked me to serve the customers their breakfast." He grumbled and kicked at dust motes floating in the sunlight. "So, I got out the trenchers and put in the porridge like she said. Didn't know they'd be so heavy."

"You put too much into the trencher. Here, let me show you how I do it."

Christopher's blue eyes grew wide as he watched me measure out two ladles of the breakfast cereal for each dish.

"That's not very much. They said they was really hungry!"

"Maybe they are hungry, but this is what they get," I said. "Remember that they get biscuits with butter as well."

"Gosh! I didn't remember the biscuits. Seems I can't do anything right," Christopher sighed and scuffed the toe of his shoe.

I tousled the boy's blond curls and bent at the waist to look him in the eye.

"First, watch your language." Christopher's cheeks reddened as I scolded him for taking the Lord's name.

"Second, it's sometimes difficult to do a chore the right way when you first try. In fact, when I started working here, I could carry only one trencher at a time, and I needed both hands to do it!"

I grabbed his hands and turned them over as if closely inspecting them. "Your hands are bigger than mine were at your age. I'll bet that you can handle a trencher in each one, provided we fill them properly."

Christopher's eyes sparkled. "Oh, yes, let me try that!"

He grabbed the ladle, dipped it into the kettle, and then carefully transported the contents to the trencher on the table. His hand wobbled a bit, and a big drop of porridge dribbled down the outside and plopped on the floor.

"Oh, no!" he cried.

"Don't worry! We'll clean it up. Watch how I do it." I dipped the ladle into the kettle, withdrew a serving, and then scraped the bottom of the ladle against the kettle's rim.

"I see!" Christopher's voice squealed with delight. He grasped the ladle delicately and carefully removed the dripping mush from the bottom. Determined not to spill a drop, he held his left hand under the oversized spoon till he reached the trencher.

"That's the way! I knew you could do it! Now, take these out and come back to fetch a plate of biscuits and butter for them, and you'll be done!"

Our young charge beamed with pride as he entered the great room to serve our guests. *Such diligence he shows as he works! He'll make a fine tavern owner someday.*

MAY 1769

Geoffrey Canfield

Paul and Eli have been watching the warehouses on Oliver's Wharf. Looks like Senhouse, Culmer, and a few others guard the crates of Madeira and tea. They haven't been able to distract the men in order to get a closer look at all the seized goods yet.

♥

"He's the perfect choice to do it, Eli. You know it. He's more than proven himself."

"We can't ask that of him. You know he'd jump at the chance. More than anything, he wants to show you that he's a good soldier."

I paced back and forth in the kitchen, feeling Molly's eyes follow me from point A to point B. Glancing up at her, I saw fear in her eyes.

"Geoffrey," she began. "This is different. This involves facing off with soldiers and guns and nobody else around to intervene. He could be injured so easily."

"And just as easily, he could excuse his being there as a boy reveling in a day free from school."

Walking over to her, I gently took her by the shoulders. "We all take chances, every day, in what we're doing to distract the general and express our distaste for this strict British rule. Paul and Eli spend hours tracking soldiers; you and Elizabeth go door to door soliciting merchants to sign the boycott. And though you haven't told me, I know you've faced down one or two soldiers while doing so."

Eli stood up. "Then, I guess the best thing is to ask him."

Molly clasped her hands together; she looked as if she were praying.

June 1769

Eli Weston

A fresh breeze blew inland from the Atlantic, moderating the stiff humidity typical in summer. We walked along Fish Street toward Long Wharf, threading our way through merchants, warehouse managers, shoppers, and out-of-work Americans seeking a day's wage.

"Every time I see all these men milling about, I get irritated," Paul groused. "The idea that British sailors can take jobs from us is, is—"

"—wrong. I know; I hear what you're saying. Feels like the King's determined to make us pay for his army one way or another."

"One of the sailors was in the tavern last night spouting off about how he gets paid from the Crown as well as the warehouse manager. Makes me burn."

"Stop! Get your hands—" A shrill scream from behind us interrupted our conversation.

Paul's face registered the alarm I felt, and we both turned and raced toward the source of the disturbance.

A young girl struggled to pull free from a man in a red coat, dragging her into an alley. The petite brunette's petticoat was torn, her gray chemise visible and ripped at the neck. She leaned away from her attacker and then swung her free hand into his ear. No sooner had she struck the man than her right foot kicked his shin.

"Ow! You stupid hedge whore; you'll pay for that!"

"Oh, no, she won't!" I shouted at the man. Now that I was closer, I could tell he was a British soldier. His face, bristling with a week's worth of whiskers, snarled at the interruption, and abruptly, he loosened his grip.

Suddenly freed, the girl whirled from her attacker and bolted toward the city. Paul and I exchanged glances, and with a nod, he quickly gave chase.

I turned slightly to the side and threw a punch, landing it squarely on the attacker's left ear. Cartilage crunched under my knuckles as the ear collapsed in on itself. Spit sprayed from his mouth, and he stumbled back. Blood flowed from the twice-hit appendage.

By the time he hit the boards, two redcoats had pushed through the gathered crowd. Each grabbed an arm. They heaved him to his feet and marched him off the wharf. Surprised they didn't nab me, I dashed after Paul and the girl. After running two blocks and not seeing either, I turned toward the tavern.

♥

"She said she didn't want to come back and talk to the guards." Paul shook his head in disgust.

"'Tis a shame she won't. Those bloody soldiers will keep harassing women as long as they aren't worried about being punished. Two redcoats happened by after the girl got away. They walked off with the offender, but you and I both know there won't be any consequences to his actions."

"What are you two talking about?" Molly approached our table with two tankards of ale.

"Nothing," Paul said. "Nothing you need to know."

"I disagree. Anything that concerns you two is important to me as well."

"Then you might as well tell her, Eli."

"You're right. She needs to know." I paused a moment to consider an appropriate way to describe the indecent behavior we'd witnessed.

"And you didn't find out who she was?" Molly asked afterward.

"She wouldn't tell me, and I didn't recognize her," Paul offered. "Probably new to the city, otherwise she wouldn't be walking the wharf alone."

"Especially now with the redcoats and their lecherous behavior."

"Paul, Eli, you surprise me. How many times am I out by myself? Going to market, to and from Anna's shop, soliciting shop owners to sign on to the boycott? Will you tell me to stay home?"

"Molly, that isn't what we're saying, but it wouldn't hurt for you to travel with one of us, or a companion, when you do those things, especially after sunset. We've warned you before; too many young women suffer from these crude attacks—"

"—and some have gone missing," Paul interrupted.

"The unspoken crime against a woman isn't to be taken lightly by anyone. We'd rather you be safe than violated in the most debased manner."

With my hands on her shoulders, I looked her in the eye to convey the truth of my words and the depth of my devotion to my only sister.

"You, above all else, must know that your brothers will always protect you."

Hester Winslow

"What in the world is he thinking?" I fumed at my husband, Cyrus. "How can he just change his mind like that? Now he's telling me that the general has his own warehouse of goods? How can I believe anything? I've already told the general that Cotton would give us all the information on Eli and Lieutenant Canfield. I've told him so many things that now I don't know whether anything I've said is true. I can't believe this has happened! I simply can't!"

Cyrus sat patiently, waiting for me to finish my diatribe. He never speaks much, but he does allow me to complete my thoughts before offering up his own. Tonight, however, he simply sat on the parlor chair and watched me pace.

"How can I face the general? What am I going to tell him?" I fell into a chair opposite my husband, rested my head on my right hand, and sighed, "Oh, that Cotton infuriates me so."

For the second time that day, I found myself waiting for a man to act. Instead, we remained seated. I quietly contemplated my predicament for the better part of an hour while waiting for Cyrus to make a suggestion or give an opinion. A rustling sound caught my attention, and I looked over at Cyrus rising from his chair. Without saying a word or even glancing my way, he left the parlor. His leaving aggravated me. My irritation grew while I stared at his receding back, and I realized that, once again, it would be up to me to turn this situation to my favor.

AUGUST 1769

GEOFFREY CANFIELD

"You can't believe that!" Eli's eyes were wide with incredulity upon hearing my explanation. "It's been nearly four years. Bridgewater's forgotten all about the black powder."

I shook my head in response. I often marveled at Eli's innate knowledge of how men and women thought, acted, and reacted, but he didn't know the general as I did. My commanding officer is a predator lying in wait, watching and making ready to pounce on unsuspecting prey. It's my intent not to become his next victim.

"Eli, the general isn't like you and me," I explained. "Sometimes I think he isn't even human. Days, even weeks, pass, and just when I feel that I can ease up and relax a bit, he says something that puts me on edge again. On days when I think back on the mill, those are the times he'll make a comment that makes me believe he knows of my involvement. I swear it's as if he has an extra sense about him! The Greeks are right—a camel never forgets its injury."

"That's just a proverb! You worry too much. You know that he's already on to another scheme to fatten his purse."

"Perhaps. But more than likely, the scheme he's onto will exact his revenge on me." I raised my eyes to his and corrected myself. "On us."

"The longer he waits, the more he can make you, or us, dance," Eli winked. "Stop worrying so much! You're exhausting me."

My friend's efforts at light-hearted banter sometimes exhaust me. Today's exchange is one of those times.

"Eli," I started and quickly retracted the thought about to leave my mouth. "I appreciate your efforts to amuse me, but this *is* a serious matter. Should he move to censure me, I could end up in a ship's brig sailing to the land of my father." I stared into his eyes to emphasize the severity of my comments. "I would lose Molly forever."

My friend rose and clapped me on the shoulder. "Then, we must continue to steer the general's thoughts in another direction. Come, let's continue to plan. Christopher's efforts were fruitful and we know that both Madeira and tea are being held in the last warehouse on

Oliver's Wharf. Chris thought he also saw one or two crates marked *linen.*"

Those words had barely been uttered when young Christopher blew through the kitchen door.

"Slow down, boy," Eli reached out a hand as if to rein in a runaway horse.

"Something bad's going to happen! I heard it from the preacher!"

Eli and I exchanged a knowing glance and wink.

I sat down to address the lad eye-to-eye. "What's going to happen and, more importantly, what preacher?"

Christopher gulped in a few deep breaths before answering. "The one at the corner of the graveyard!"

I knew the fellow. He hung around the gravestones of Increase Mather and his son, Cotton, both buried in Copp's Hill Burying Ground, the highest point in north Boston. One could find the preacher late at night slinking around the graves, muttering to himself and waving his shapeless black felt hat gripped with misshapen, arthritic fingers.

Eli chuckled and reassured Christopher. "Don't give him a second thought. With his addled mind, he doesn't know what he's saying."

"But you have to hear him. It's the truth! It really is. He said we're all going to die! Please, Geoffrey, please go and listen. Then, you'll know I'm telling you the truth!"

"Then, so we shall. Eli, care to join me for an evening walk?"

"Whatever that preacher's sermonizing, he sure has little Chris in a pother." Eli's hands vigorously rubbed his scalp.

"Careful, my friend, or you'll find yourself with a pate as shiny as your father's."

We turned left and passed Revere's house and followed Prince Street for a couple of blocks. In the distance, we heard a high, nasal voice piercing the air. Through the twilight, we espied the wiry figure gesticulating wildly. By the time we had drawn within fifty feet, we could decipher his words:

"The Creator of the heavens, our most merciful God, fashioned the sun, the moon, the stars. He created these harbingers of the future to bring us closer to Him. These bright stars with their tails, their glorious tails! Shedding their evil behind them, raining their evil upon us. Look around you. Can't you see it already? The pox is in Charleston. Charleston! What else will we have to endure?"

Eli shouted in response, "Old man, go to bed! You're frightening people."

"But it is true, young man. The pox is in Charleston today. Soon it will be in Boston. Many will die!"

Eli had survived the pox, so I knew that his reply would be a proper rebuke.

"Old man, don't worry about the comet. It has not caused the pox. And it has no bearing on whether the pox will spread."

The preacher's eyes grew wide, and he shook a crooked finger at my friend. "You, *you* are ignorant of the glorious heavens and God's omens, which are visible for all to see if you open your eyes and ears to His Word."

"Come on, Eli," I gently tugged at my friend's elbow. "Begone, preacher! Cease your speculating. You are vexing the children with your ideas. Go home. Sleep."

The preacher's fury at being run off wasn't abated. As we turned our backs, his admonishment struck hard. "Heed my warning: this beauteous star that shines brightly in the sky holds no goodness for you. For neither of you."

After a final draft of beer back at The Three Lions, I thought no more of the preacher, comets, or predictions of pestilence. The next morning, however, Christopher's voice echoed in my mind as I read the *Gazette.* "The preacher is right," he had said. And a small notice submitted by the town clerk confirmed it: the pox was in Boston, near Griffin's Wharf, and in the western part of the city.

September 1769

MOLLY WESTON

"What's that you're reading?"

Mother sat next to the hearth, stirring a bubbling pot with one hand. She gave me the piece of paper and smiled widely.

"Our spinning contest is coming together nicely. This is one more reply to our missive, from Dedham."

"Just in time, I'd say. Burlington, Concord, Lexington, Waltham, Framingham," I counted participating towns on my fingers. "Who else?"

"Don't forget Lynn and Quincy. Oh, and Middletown."

Earlier, Mother and Anna sent letters to surrounding towns suggesting a spinning contest to increase support for wearing homespun clothing. Women throughout the Bay Colony responded positively to our idea to support the nonimportation agreement and boycott of European clothing. Each group of townswomen selected a minister to measure and track the skeins of thread and yarn, and the contest would last six days.

"How many women in Boston are spinning?"

"As of yesterday, we have one hundred forty-eight pledged to spin."

"So few?"

"Molly! That's a wonderful number of women! Not everyone can leave their homes to participate. Even so, we have many more who pledged at least one day of spinning."

As is typical, Mother was right. On Monday, nearly two hundred women carried their spinning wheels to churches throughout Boston, where they made full use of sanctuary benches and aisles. A few dared to set their wheels on the border of the Common, in full view of drilling British regulars. Mother and I chose to spin at the Cockerel Church as it was closer than West Church, where we attended on Sundays.

"What a sight they make!" commented Eli after dinner on Wednesday as we lingered over the table. "Every morning and every night, women all over the city, carrying their wheels through the city."

"A most peculiar parade, if you ask me," added Paul.

"Nobody asked you!" I retorted. My brothers and their comments exasperated me. "Not everyone is free to roam the city after dark and carve the number forty-five into doorways. We need to voice our opinions, too, but have to do it in other ways. Furthermore, unlike you men, our resistance is productive."

"Oh, ho!" Paul and Eli laughed at my attempt at humor. "And how productive will you, fair ladies of Boston, be? Just how many skeins will you produce for the city's consumption?"

"Our women will best the others," I boasted.

"I hope so. Peter Oliver is holding court over at Monck's Tavern and saying your spinning contest is just 'another scheme'[6] to keep the Colony agitated."

"We shall see. The women are dedicated." Mother's soft voice startled us, and I smiled at her endorsement.

♥

For six days, we completed early morning tavern duties and then headed out the kitchen door to Gallups Alley and up to Middle Street. Cockerel Church, named for the rooster weathervane decorating its spire, was one block east. There, we pumped treadles and spun till our forefingers and thumbs burned and blistered. And when they bled, we wrapped them in linen strips torn from rags and continued to spin. At dusk, we carted our wheels back to the tavern, tended to supper and evening duties, and eventually retired to a well-earned slumber.

By the end of Friday evening, the Cockerel spinners had produced 47 skeins. I was anxious to learn what the week's total would be. On Saturday, we would add our totals with those of the other churches.

♥

It was mid-September, and I looked up from folding handkerchiefs when I heard the shop door open. Hester crossed the threshold and closed the door. Her eyes swept the room before she offered a greeting.

"Good morning," I hesitantly replied. During her previous visit to Anna's shop, Hester had purchased a lovely blue petticoat. I noticed she wasn't wearing it today, and briefly wondered which of our offerings she might fancy, if any. Her outer garment, made of finely spun linen, featured an obvious European import—Irish lace trim.

"May I show you some of our kerchiefs or shawls?"

"No, thank you. Actually, I came to ask you to coffee."

My fingers fumbled, and I dropped the delicate kerchief on the floor. I stooped to gather it as she continued.

"I thought it would be nice for us to spend more time together. Like we used to when we were children."

Anna interrupted our conversation. "Why, what a sweet idea, Hester." I turned at hearing my employer's voice calling out from the back. She strode into the main room and stood beside me.

"Molly, I can spare you this afternoon." Anna pressed her hand on my back and gently guided me toward the door. "You deserve a little time. Why don't you two go now?"

The entire exchange had taken but a minute, and soon I found myself walking with Hester, who chattered incessantly. Anna always thought the best of everyone, but she didn't bear the scars of Hester's barbed tongue as I did.

"Molly! Are you even listening?"

"Oh, sorry. I was thinking of Anna letting me have the afternoon free."

"Isn't it wonderful?" she chirped.

"Hmm? Yes, wonderful."

Hester opened the door to the British Coffee House. At two o'clock in the afternoon, most patrons had returned to work or home, and I viewed many empty choice window tables. My companion's selection, however, sat in the middle of the room, far from the windows where I could have gazed and daydreamed while the magpie sang.

"Lovely," I mumbled tonelessly while placing my purse on my lap.

"Two coffees, please." Hester placed our order with the server. "I'm so glad we can have this time together."

I didn't know what to say, so I simply nodded.

"The *Post* reported that Boston women spun nearly forty thousand skeins. How impressive!"

"Actually, *we* spun forty thousand two hundred fifty-two."

"My, my, that is wonderful. I'm not good at figures, as you know. I mean, why would I need to know all that? Cyrus is so adept at ciphering that there is no occasion for me to use that knowledge."

"Of course." I remembered Hester's education concentrated on coquetry rather than reading and arithmetic. *At least, she's a bit self-aware of that lack.*

"Cyrus gives me an allowance, which I'm free to spend as I wish. Speaking of spending, what does Anna have in stock that would accentuate my new blue petticoat?"

The afternoon dragged on through two cups each of steaming cream-laced beverages as my companion narrated an endless review of European fashions. The tone of her voice caught my attention when she veered into an unexpected topic.

"Such a pity you have those scars on your wrists. You never told me why Jack and Salmon abducted you."

Her non-question query made me tug on my sleeves to hide the pale rings, then I stopped when I realized it made no sense to try to hide them. They had been noticed. I breathed in, exhaled, and sighed in resignation.

"Some years ago, well, not quite that long ago." My mind worked to find a short explanation that wouldn't compromise anyone, yet steer Hester into the same tack that Cotton was using.

"How is it I haven't heard what happened?" Hester leaned in, placed her chin on folded hands, and looked at me intently.

She had cornered me. My cheeks pinked while I searched my mind for a suitable response.

"I'm not really sure why they did it. I knew them as patrons of The Three Lions." It was good to stay as true as possible to what happened. Jack and Salmon had frequented the tavern. I wasn't about to tell her that I had been eavesdropping on their conversation about the general's hoards of black powder.

"Oh, Molly. *Quelle horreur!* That must have been a terrible experience."

"They tied my hands—the scars are what's left of the time I spent captive."

Hester patted my hand in a comforting gesture. "I'm so sorry that happened." She almost sounded sincere.

"How did you escape?"

Oh, how I wish I could escape these questions!

"They tied me to a post in a barn. I used a protruding nail like a saw to cut through the rope. Anyway, after some time, I got free."

"You're *so* courageous. I don't know that I could have survived such an ordeal."

That supercilious tone again. *You probably would have fainted immediately.*

She looked pensive for a moment, and I detected a trace of biting doubt in her voice. "And nobody helped you?"

Is it a lie if I shake my head and don't say anything?

October 1769

GEOFFREY CANFIELD

I wadded up the order and threw it at the wall, nearly hitting Molly as she opened the door to my room.

"Oh, my!" She backed out quickly.

"My apologies, Molly. Come in. I'm annoyed, that's all. But not at you! Colonel Dalrymple and his orders."

Buttermilk batted the paper ball across the room and then suddenly flopped on the floor next to the table. Molly moved through the room and sat on the lone chair, patiently awaiting more explanation. She reached down to scratch Buttermilk's cheeks, who purred in appreciation. The domestic scene made me smile.

"We've been ordered not to respond to the insults, but it's getting more difficult to control the men."

A moue spoiled my love's face. "You can't expect us not to do what we can to make their lives miserable."

"Molly, you will do what you will." She routinely demonstrated inner strength that was missing in some of my own troops. "There's no denying you, but it's not enough that I agree with your position. A thin border between what I think and what I do shadows me constantly. The duplicity wears on me. I'd sooner join you and insult soldiers than continue this charade."

"Then why don't you leave the Army? Obviously, that is what you want to do."

"Not yet. Not without an income."

Molly rolled her eyes and sighed. "You always have the same response. When will it be time to leave?" Her eyes widened. "*Will* it ever be time?"

"Yes, and please don't think it won't. It's a matter of finding an officer who'll purchase my commission. Only by selling it can I leave and purchase the farmland."

"Surely, enough ensigns are willing to step up in rank."

"But I need to know the individual well. This isn't a traditional acquisition; I must be confident that the purchaser won't question my motives."

"But it's no secret that we see one another. We're not the only mixed couple in Boston. Plenty of young women keep company with the British."

"But they don't know the depth of our feelings. Most of Boston's young women keep company with the British because it's fashionable. To sell my commission and return home—that's an action they will understand. To sell it and then side with the patriots or, as they call them, Yankees, that will put us in danger."

Eli Weston

I rubbed my eyes—a useless effort meant to ease the frustration boiling over in my soul. A slap on my back forced my eyes up. William Molineux settled next to me on the bench.

"What bedevils you?"

Before I could answer, John Hancock and Drs. Young and Warren walked through the tavern doors and joined us in the back of the great room.

Hancock's typically placid face pinched in anger; his red-splotched cheeks contrasted with his deep blue coat of finely spun wool. His dark eyes stormed with inner fury. "It's unheard of!" he hissed.

Conversation paused as Paul approached with a tray of ale. He placed the tankards on the end of the table and quickly left to tend to other customers. He and I had already discussed tonight's topic, and his task during this intimate meeting was to ensure other customers kept their distance from us.

I distributed the mugs, and we all took a long drink, forcing a calming pause on the group.

Hancock looked each of us in the eye. "How can Bernard ignore Otis for the position of Chief Justice?"

"Ignoring one man's qualifications to assure a crony's ascension is troubling," Warren agreed.

Young shook his head and sighed. "Replacing Thomas Hutchison as chief justice is quite the promotion for Peter Oliver. Once you add the disgraced Andrew Oliver to those two, we face a never-ending triumvirate of office grabbers. My head spins when I think about it."

"The intermarriage of the Oliver and Hutchinson families gives us a formidable enemy," Hancock continued. "With Hutchinson backing the governor, Andrew in the upper house, and now Peter heading the Judicature, our lives are governed by an ever-smaller cadre. Isn't it enough that they line their fat purses with our taxes?"

"There's no end to their greed," interrupted Warren. "What steps can we take to counteract this breach of trust?"

Young twirled his mug on a ring of moisture. "Unfortunately, there is no recourse available to us. Bernard's action is final. We, the non-conforming colonists, have to abide by his ill-formed decision."

♥

"Mein's done it again!" I slapped the *Boston Chronicle* on the table in disgust.

"Who's listed in this issue?" Geoffrey picked up the newspaper and glanced at the front page.

"Does it really matter? Why do he and Fleming publish these names? Mein doesn't even check to see whether the men have signed the non-importation agreement. How many times has he published a merchant's name, someone whose shipment was ordered before he signed the agreement?"

"Why should he bother to check?" Geoffrey countered. "Mein's loyalty to Britain is his newspaper's anchor. He uses these names to build support for the Crown, and by extension, the Board of Commissioners. It's all public information. All he need do is stop by the Customs House to see what ships have arrived and review their bills of lading."

My friend shook out the broadsheet's creases and scanned the print. "I rather think he enjoys playing the nuisance." He then pulled out a copy of the latest *Gazette.*

"This will make you feel better. Ben's been countering Mein's heinous efforts. This week must be the fourth time Mein's listed as a non-signer. And William Palfrey is writing letters again. This time, he's ridiculing Mein for not signing because he supports so many people in his print shop and at home. Listen:

> So rather than let 17 people do other work than his, he would ruin and make slaves, like some other tyrants of his kind, all those of the same business in the country, who had so much publick spirit, rather to suffer themselves than see their country in slavery."[7]

"Eli! Eli!" An immature voice interrupted.

"Come on in, Chris."

Geoffrey and I invited the young boy into my room. Our plan was to task him with a second trial. He'd proven himself useful in tracking Cotton's efforts with Hester, but now we would be testing his artfulness and cleverness.

"Are you sure you can do this?" I looked at the lad who'd insisted he could help the Sons of Liberty.

"Yessir!" Christopher stood straight and tall, as tall as a boy of little more than four feet could reach.

Geoffrey placed his hands on the boy's shoulders and crouched down to look him in the eyes.

"You'll be our ears and our eyes, Christopher." The boy nodded. "It's important that you observe and listen, but also remember what you see and hear. We need to know who the Customs House informant is. Are you sure you can do this?"

He vigorously nodded.

I smiled at the lad's earnestness. "Be careful. Be watchful of others. You may not be the only spy. Remember, the Loyalists may have their own eyes on watch."

"Yessir!"

"Don't get caught."

"Ah, Eli, you know that won't happen. I'm too fast. I can outrun those old people. I bet I could even find that guy who slit his wife's throat before anybody else."

Chris had recently read of James Hedges, a Lexington resident who murdered his wife. It was a horrifically brutal offense, sending women into nervous fits and putting many men in town on watch for the man wearing blue plush breeches. "I think you should concentrate on this task rather than Hedges. Remember, you may be faster, but if there are more of them and they're working together, you could be surrounded before you could escape."

"Oh, geez." Christopher scuffed his boot on the floorboard. "Well, I s'pose that could happen. I'll watch out. I promise!"

"Then get along. We'll see you at supper."

Christopher grinned widely and flew out the door. We listened to his feet thumping down the steps and then a crash of crockery hitting the floor. Curses bounced up the narrow stairway, trailed by a high-pitched voice. "Scuse me! I gotta go!"

Geoffrey's eyes caught mine, and we burst into laughter.

"Our little spy needs to be more circumspect with his demeanor if he is to succeed," he said with a smile.

"My bones tell me he'll be fine."

Geoffrey goodheartedly jabbed me in the ribs. "Your bones? We're relying on intangible intelligence now?"

I shook my head and crossed my arms. "No, it's just a feeling. Have you ever seen such a politically insightful head on someone so young? He pays attention to everything, and he thinks about what he sees and hears."

"Intelligent he is, but I'm hoping he conquers his impetuosity. The wrong word spoken at an inopportune moment, and…" his voice trailed off.

I nodded in agreement. The search and seizure of Hancock's ship last year surprised us, and now Malcolm's warehouse searched twice in as many years. The Customs Board was abusing its authority, and John Mein was an integral part of the Board's campaign against the non-importation agreement.

♥

Two weeks later, Christopher ran into The Three Lions. His cheeks, ruddy from the cold temperature, and his nose, dripping with mucous, faded from view when I saw his wild eyes. They hurriedly scanned the room till they landed on my own. Their intensity gave me pause, and my jaw clenched. *He has news of the informer!*

Lest afternoon tipplers show an abnormally piqued interest, I met the boy halfway through the great room and, fearing he would blurt out the name prematurely, ushered him into the kitchen. His chin trembled, and tears welled up as he looked at me.

"Chris, tell me what's going on. Did anyone hurt you?" My eyes quickly scanned him for torn clothes or scrapes while my hands palpated him for swollen or dislocated joints.

He shook his head and hiccoughed briefly as he attempted an answer.

"No. It's not me. It's Cap'n Malcolm."

"What's happened? Take a deep breath. Now, tell me."

"Cap'n Malcolm, Eli." Tears previously held back now poured from the child's eyes. "He's dead."

The news hit me like a punch in the gut, and I gasped. Molly stepped over and placed her hand on my shoulder. "Sit. Now."

I lowered myself to the bench next to Chris, who sidled up to me. Placing my arm around his shoulders to make him feel better comforted me as well. In my mind, I saw Daniel standing with me and the other Sons of Liberty against soldiers, and later, customs workers, to protest warehouse raids. In his personal life, he worked hard and rose through the ranks of seamanship to become a captain, finally moving onto land as a merchant.

While images of Daniel's life played through my mind, Geoffrey entered the back door. He took in the somber faces, "So, you've heard."

As she approached her beau, Molly said, "Chris told us. Do you know how?"

"Not really." Geoffrey caressed her face and then looked at me. "My bones tell me the power of the Customs Board of Commissioners assessed a deadly toll."

I rubbed my eyes to hide emerging tears, but my voice choked me. "He was only forty-four."[8]

"It was the preacher's doing," Christopher sobbed. "He said we'd all pay."

I drew the child close. "No, Chris, it wasn't the preacher. We don't know why he died, but it wasn't because of anything the preacher said."

November 1769

Molly Weston

"Hush!" I raised my finger to my lips. "Don't talk nonsense."

Geoffrey circled the kitchen in his long stride. "I should be paying my respects to Daniel, not ordering troops about the city." Four paces, turn, three paces, turn, four paces. Watching the man made me dizzy.

Worried that he would call unwanted attention to himself by attending Daniel Malcolm's funeral, I lowered my voice and sternly admonished him. "You'll do what your commanding officer requires of you, and nothing," I raised my hand to halt his interruption, "nothing else."

A door creaked behind us, and we turned to see Christopher sneak into the kitchen.

"I almost surprised you! If it weren't for that door making a noise… "

I tousled the boy's golden locks. "Let's get Father to see to that hinge."

For the first time, he pulled back and began to comb his hair with his fingers. "Don't do that, Molly. I'm too old for that now."

I peeked at Geoffrey, the corners of my mouth turning up. I opened my mouth to respond to the imp, but Geoffrey shook his head. Feeling a bit reproved, I tended the stew bubbling over the hearth.

Addressing the lad, Geoffrey quickly shifted roles from army lieutenant to teacher. "When you're on a mission and need to enter a building, you won't know whether a door will creak when you come upon it. What if I had been a commissioner, or one of his agents?"

Chris puffed up his chest and faced his instructor. "I'd tell him I got confused, that I was in the wrong building," he cockily replied.

"What if he doesn't believe you? Better to ensure your safety ahead of time." The newly minted professor purposefully strode toward the door and mimed his actions. "Carry some animal fat or suet with you. Rub it onto the hinge to cut the noise."

The pupil asked, "And use it every time?"

Geoffrey's eyes twinkled as he nodded. "The city of Boston will have the quietest doors in the colony."

"Molly," Geoffrey turned his attention to me, "could you spare a small box or bottle? Fill it with some of that bacon fat."

I chuckled as I filled one of the smaller bottles with some of the viscous liquid and stoppered it with a cork. "Be sure you don't get too close to the pigs with fat in your pocket," I warned Christopher. "When they get a whiff of this, the hogs may want their own revenge!"

"Thanks. This'll be helpful." Christopher solemnly stuffed the bottle into his pocket. "Oh, I almost forgot! I found this." He pulled out a crumpled sheet of paper and smoothed it out on the table.

Geoffrey and I leaned over to view the specimen. Geoffrey squinted, snatched up the sheet, and examined it closely.

Geoffrey's eyes didn't leave the paper. "Where did you get this?"

"Well, I, uh, I found it."

"Did you? Hmmm. Exactly where did you find it? On the street perhaps?"

The boy's cheeks reddened, and he began to stammer. "Oh, yes, that was it. On the street."

The teacher peered over the top of the paper to dress down his student. "I think not, young man."

Christopher's stature shrank at hearing those words. In an instant, he'd reverted to the little street urchin we'd taken under our care.

"Maybe it wasn't on the street," he began. After a few scuffs of his boot, he sighed, "On the general's desk."

"General Bridgewater's desk?" Geoffrey shushed me with a raised hand, signaling my voice shouldn't be more than a whisper. I settled down but hissed, "Whatever moved you to enter his home? Have you no sense of the danger you were in?"

"I'll ask you the same," Geoffrey added. "What was your purpose?"

The spy-in-training straightened his spine. "I hadn't found out anything about a spy at the Customs House, so I asked myself, 'What would Eli do?' Eli always has a second plan, so I needed a second plan too. I thought and thought, and then I knew. The man the spy reported to would know who the spy is!"

Geoffrey narrowed his eyes and looked the lad up and down. "Thus, you decided to trespass and rifle through the general's belongings?"

"Only his office, sir. My hands were shaking so much that I didn't want to spend a lot of time there."

Geoffrey flaunted the paper at Christopher. "Good thing, that conscience of yours. Eli and I'll talk about this tonight."

After feeding Christopher and sending him on his way, it was my turn to learn what he, and now Geoffrey, found keenly interesting about that piece of paper.

He passed the script across the table for me to read. "It's notes, Molly, in General Bridgewater's handwriting."

As I scanned the document, I realized its impact. Not only was the informer named, but a list of names ended the notes.

"Why are these men listed?"

"Not only men, Molly. Look deeper into the names; there are a few women shopkeepers as well."

Seeing the name of Elizabeth Murray, I nodded. Elizabeth, now on her third husband and having richly profited from the death of each, was a firm believer that girls should be brought up to be industrious individuals. As such, she financed Ame and Betsy Cumming's millinery. To my knowledge, all three women had more in common with Anna, Mother, and me than, say, Hester. Then the reason behind the series sprang to mind.

"This is a list of future raids, isn't it?"

"I'm afraid so." He tapped his finger on the page. "Notice that the general crossed out Daniel Malcolm's name."

"No reason to raid a merchant who's departed this life. Still," I paused, "these words distress me."

"Giving you a reason to despair?"

"No, not that. It's more a sense of discouragement. When the King recalled the Stamp Act, my heart filled with hope and happiness. I truly believed that he understood our position and would allow us to govern ourselves. Separate—"

"—yet still loyal to the King?"

"Exactly. And now, we, they," I sighed. "What point can be made if neither side is willing to listen to the other's arguments?"

"Contentious debate accompanied by vengeful acts by both parties. I fear we have reached an impasse." Geoffrey rose, leaned across the table, and kissed my forehead. "Our fate lies in the hands of others. However, I believe that you and I still have parts to play in determining our own future."

December 1769

Geoffrey Canfield

"How did he win?"

Ever since Christopher pilfered the list of upcoming raids from General Bridgewater's desk, he's pestered me about military history. Eli's father, Jonathan, who fought in the French and Indian War, has regaled him with tales of skirmishes and heroic deeds of brave American soldiers. From me, he's wanted to know more about the British officers who led the larger battles and sieges. Tonight, he sat cross-legged on my bed, absorbing every detail about the Battle of Quebec.

His question about Major General James Wolfe required a lengthy response.

"It was 1759, and the general had orders to capture Quebec City. That spring, he organized his troops, and they sailed up the St. Lawrence River. In late June, they reached Île d'Orléans."

"What? I don't understand when you talk French."

"Orleans Island—across the river from the city."

"Why didn't you just say that?"

I drilled my eyes into his and continued the saga. "Unfortunately for the general, the Marquis de Montcalm had already established his French and Canadian troops along the cliffs overlooking the St. Lawrence.

"General Wolfe organized a battery of cannons across the river from the city, but barrage after barrage didn't lure out Montcalm's troops, although it nearly destroyed lower Quebec."

"Didn't he want to fight?"

"You have to think of it from his point of view, Chris. If Montcalm and his troops are in a superior position, which being up high is, then there's no reason to give up that advantage. The only time you'd need to meet the enemy is if you were surrounded, under siege, and your provisions were scarce. But that wasn't the situation for Montcalm."

"So, General Wolfe had to figure out another plan."

"Correct. For weeks, Wolfe's troops endured hot summer temperatures, humidity so dense that their clothes never dried, and bugs so thick you'd have to chew them if you breathed through your mouth. The men began to fall ill; dysentery and other diseases spread throughout the troops, thinning their ranks. Even the general became ill. Nevertheless, he grew impatient, and on July 31, he ordered an assault on the east side of the city, along Beauport shore."

"But weren't the soldiers too tired or sick to fight?"

"Of course, but Major General Wolfe believed that attacking before he lost more men would be better. War won't always wait for everything to be perfect."

"How'd he convince the soldiers to attack?"

"I imagine he gave a rousing speech, telling them how important it was to win, how they needed to ignore their pain and fight their fatigue."

"Kind of like working till you're so tired you can't work no more?"

"Exactly like that, Chris. If you can exert that much effort, your reward is not having to repeat the work later. In this case, work is another battle, or at the very least, a longer one."

"So, what happened?"

"The general misjudged the condition of his troops. The French and Canadians hadn't suffered any illness, so they were in better shape to fight. Although our soldiers fought valiantly, they couldn't advance their position."

"And Montcalm's troops held the cliffs. They fired on the British troops below. The superior position, right?"

"Yes, and the battle dragged on for weeks—the entire month of August."

"That's a long time to fight if you're tired."

"Indeed." I lowered my voice for effect. "At the end of the month, the general and his brigadiers devised a new plan. They'd cross the river and attack Quebec from the west side. From this position, they could scale the cliffs more easily."

Christopher leaned forward. He, too, was whispering. "And?"

"This attack went better. A scouting group climbed the slope and happened upon a small French garrison, which they captured."

"That cleared the way for the others?"

"Essentially. The battle was fought outside the city on a plateau and lasted only an hour or so."

"And the general became a hero?"

"In a way. He was wounded during the battle."

"Really?"

I nodded. "Three times. He died from those wounds, but he wasn't the only one."

"Soldiers?"

"Of course, but I was speaking of the Marquis de Montcalm. He, too, suffered a severe wound and died the following day. Within a week of that assault, Quebec City fell to the British."

My young student fell silent and clasped and unclasped his hands, stretching his fingers long and wide.

"Chris?"

"Just thinking." He cocked his head and looked up at me. "We don't have any superior position, and I don't think we can starve out the British, but maybe we can make them want to leave."

Later that night, I relayed Chris's cryptic comment to Eli. "He's onto something. Not sure what, but he's making plans."

Eli threw his hands into the air. "He's eleven! What can an eleven-year-old do to hurt thousands of British soldiers?"

"You, Eli," I pointed at my friend, "were the one to alert me to his intelligence. He's proving himself in all sorts of ways. Lately, he's a disciple of military history. I don't know why he's suddenly interested in how battles are fought and won, but the two of us need to figure out what trouble he's crafting before he gets into danger."

January 1770

Eli Weston

After Christopher stole the list from General Bridgewater, Eli and I agreed that the lad should avoid both the Customs House and the general's quarters. I soon learned, however, that Christopher didn't know the meaning of the word *avoid*.

Chris hurried through his morning chore of clearing the tables. Trenchers clattered, and bits of food splattered the kitchen floor as he hurriedly flung the eating implements onto the sideboard. After a quick wipe-down of the great room's tables, he ran for the door, nearly knocking Molly off her feet as he left for school.

Molly rearranged her mobcap and apron as she entered the kitchen. "What's his hurry? Lately, he has no time for anything other than chores. Time was he'd sit and chat with Mother and me. I'd have to order him to class."

I shrugged. "He's been rather secretive since we coopted him as a junior spy. I told him to stay away from the general's office, but I'm not sure he's doing that."

My sister lifted the ladle from the water bucket and waved it at me, spraying cold liquid in my face. "You don't know what he's doing? You're supposed to be the one protecting him!" She tossed the ladle back in and muttered, "I can't begin to tell you what I think of you and Geoffrey using a small boy like that for your own purposes."

Duly chastised, I brought up the matter to Geoffrey that evening. We agreed that, between the two of us and with Paul as backup, we could follow Christopher during the hours he wasn't in school or at The Three Lions. I would take the first shift in the morning.

I waited in the alley about ten feet from the kitchen door, wishing I could clap my hands and stomp my feet to fight off the winter air, but I didn't dare make a noise. The dark shadows stretching over the tight squeeze of brick buildings frozen from last night's temperature hid me from the boy leaving the tavern. At the alley entrance, he turned right towards Fish Street, and I began my pursuit.

Morning shoppers ambled along the street, stopping to chat with friends and merchants, and I weaved in and out of workers and artisans as they loaded and unloaded their wares for the day's business. Frosty breath and steaming horses and cattle obscured my view. My short quarry was quick of foot, and his blond crown disappeared, reappearing in unexpected places. I wondered if he sensed he was being trailed and felt a bit of pride at how well he'd perfected his skills.

At King Street, I watched Christopher turn towards the school. Sighing with relief that he hadn't made his way to the Customs House or General Bridgewater's headquarters, I traced my route back to The Three Lions.

February 1770

Geoffrey Canfield

"No, Molly, Christopher hasn't been back to the Customs House. None of us has seen him there." We were sharing a cup of coffee in the tavern kitchen when she broached the subject of Christopher's extracurricular activities.

"How can you be sure? For all you know, he walks in the front door of the schoolhouse and slips out the back. You're always saying how clever he is."

I rubbed my face in frustration, then lifted my eyes to look at my beloved. *Her heart is so filled with affection for this boy!* I sighed. "You're right. Maybe we've not been as diligent as Chris is artful."

Molly took my hands in hers as she moved closer to me on the bench. "I don't want to see him hurt. He's taken to learning and knows the meaning of being a responsible person. I truly think he will make a success of himself."

I gently kissed her forehead and leaned mine against it. "He'll be fine. The lad knows what to do regardless of the situation."

She sighed. "Do we know that for sure? Or do we think he has the knowledge and skill when he really doesn't?"

The door burst open, and startled, Molly and I pulled apart.

Young Christopher, oblivious to our intimate posture, crossed the threshold apace, wielding a seventeen-by-twenty-four-inch broadsheet in his left hand. "Look what I found!"

I wondered whether he really did *find* the paper or pilfered it from the general or some other officer. He laid it on the table and proudly stepped back so we could admire it.

A border of laurel leaves, swords, and furled banners surrounded a nine-by-twelve-inch engraving of Major General James Wolfe. Below the portrait, General George Townshend and Vice Admiral Charles Saunders reviewed details of the Battle of Quebec City.

"Who gave you this?" I asked, knowing that the cost of such a broadsheet would be far above whatever his meager pay from The Three Lions could afford.

"Down on the docks. One of the soldiers was reading it out loud when I stopped by. I told him that bit about the garrison up on the hill, and he gave me the paper. Said if I knew so much about the battle, I should have it."

"Then I guess you should keep it." I passed the sheet back to the boy.

Chris folded the large paper till it was a palm-sized box and stuffed it into his pants pocket. He patted the bulging fabric at his hip. "I'll keep it safe."

Christopher Snider

Molly keeps trying to teach me, but learning is so dull. She gave me some paper and told me to write down what I think because I need to practice my writing. I don't know what she means by thots, so every night I'll put down what I did. Maybe that will make her happy.

Today, I left the tavern but didn't go to school. I spent the morning at Hutchinson Wharf. Nothing to report.

Today, I went to school. Mister Conrad broke two quills and almost cursed out loud. He whacked me on the back of the hand for laughing. That's all.

I'm not sure whether I'm doing this writing right.

Today was fun! On my way to school, I saw General Bridgewater on the other side of the street, so I turned around and followed him. I practiced my spying. He went into the British Coffeehouse. I had coins enough for a cup of coffee, so I went in too. The owner looked really busy with the general. I wanted to hear what they were saying, so I knelt down and fussed with my boot buckle, making it look like it was broken and I was fixin it.

The owner said, "How much?"

And the general said, "Two crates."

Then the owner said, "When will I have it?"

The general said he'd deliver tomorrow. Then he kicked my foot and told me to get out of the way. Then I went to tell Eli.

Eli Weston

When I walked into the tavern, Paul motioned me over to the corner table where Christopher spooned stew into his gob. Gravy and bits of carrot dribbled from the corners of his mouth as he greeted me with a waving spoon.

"Eli! Over here!"

My brother's voice pierced the tavern's buzzing hubbub. I smiled at Chris's enthusiasm for food and sat across the table from the voracious youngster.

"You'll never guess what I found out."

"You're probably right. Looks as if you're rather hungry. Why not finish your stew first?"

Paul set a trencher and a tankard in front of me. Steam from roasted vegetables in a beefy sauce floated a delicious aroma that tickled my hunger. "Mmm. Now I know why you're eating so fast."

"Mmm," Christopher's head bobbed as he mumbled through a mouthful of the hearty soup.

Molly appeared behind him with her own trencher and spoon. She instructed Chris, "Don't talk with your mouth full," and then sat down next to him. "It's good manners to chew, swallow, and then speak."

Chris nodded obediently, gulped, and then told us of his day's activities. "What do you think he was talking about?"

"The general? Well, you haven't given us much information, but what you have provided holds promise. Whatever it is, we know that the owner of the British Coffee House wants two crates. What comes in crates that a coffeehouse operator will want?"

Molly's spoon scraped the bottom of her trencher as she scooped up the last bite-sized potato. Before carrying it to her mouth, she looked at me and said flatly, "Tea."

Christopher's excitement forced him out of his seat. "Yes!"

"Shush!" Molly motioned him back onto the bench.

Christopher hunched over his food like a dog with a bone. His eyes gleamed with excitement as he dredged a biscuit through the gravy sticking to the trencher's sides. "I'm not going to school tomorrow," he announced.

Molly's eyebrows arched, and she addressed her concern to me. "Is that such a good idea? Isn't this something that you or Paul could look into?"

"Actually, it makes sense to have Chris do some of the initial exploration. Once we have confirmation, then we'll get Paul, Geoffrey, and maybe some others involved. It's easier for Chris to run into the general and blame it on circumstance than for one of us to explain our presence to him repeatedly."

I leaned across the table and playfully punched the lad in the bicep. "Right?"

Chris stood to return the jab, nearly knocking his trencher into Molly's lap. "Right!" He quickly grabbed the vessel and, with a sheepish look at her, sat down.

She laughed. "Go on, now. Clear off these tables. Sounds like you'll have a big day tomorrow."

♥

Paul and I passed few people on the street as we slowly made our way to the British Coffee House. My younger brother blew on his hands and clapped them together. "Any reason our visit couldn't have waited till tomorrow? May not be warmer, but at least we'd be able to spot the ice before we slip."

A cold wind blew in from the Atlantic and down our necks as we turned the final corner to the establishment. "We have more of a reason to be going out tonight than if we stopped by during the day. Let's see who's in the mood to talk this evening, shall we?"

I opened the door and followed Paul into the great room. We shivered in unison when the coffeehouse's warm air firmly embraced us. I found two seats near some red-coated soldiers and men we knew to be loyal to the governor and made my way to the table. My cheeks tingled as the skin thawed, and my fingers ached to wrap around a steaming mug of coffee.

Paul unbuttoned his coat and moved to hang it on a rack near a table of men engaged in lively debate. Their voices carried, two tables hence, although the buzz of other conversations muddied the words. Paul paused, looking as if he were about to join the group, then slowly pivoted and returned to our table.

He chuckled as he swung his leg over the bench and clamped two hands around his own stoneware mug.

My brows knit in confusion. "What's so funny?"

"Nothing really. It's the realization that Christopher is right on the mark with his information."

"Unexpected from someone so young?"

"Perhaps. I keep thinking of him as the little ragamuffin playing with Boots."

It was my turn to chuckle. "Exactly what did you hear over there?" I motioned to the raucous table to my left.

"The chests of tea. They're fighting over how to divide the spoils. Judging by the intensity of their discussion, you'd think it was pirate gold."

"Might as well be. The owner openly serves tea, despite the boycott, and I'd bet he makes a pretty penny on every cup he sells. His patrons are here specifically because they're served the *bloody stuff.*"

Paul laughed aloud at my attempt to sound British. "We've heard what we came to learn. Are you warm enough to head home?"

Geoffrey Canfield

The sun tried hard, but gray clouds blocked its rays from warming the city. Goose flesh covered my bones beneath my woolen coat, and I longed to be indoors, sitting by a roaring fire and warming my frozen feet. Thoughts of my future with Molly occupied my mind as I patrolled the streets. Drawing nearer the Customs House, I came across pedestrians and a few horses running away from the building.

An angry voice called out, "You again!" followed by a squeal of pain.

I pushed through the crowd to disrupt the scuffle, but drew back when I saw the assailant—Ebenezer Richardson. Within a split second, even before I could see him, I knew the squeal came from Christopher.

"Let go of me!" Christopher screamed. "You've no right!"

"I've every right! You've been spying on me!"

By this time, I'd reached the combatants and pulled Christopher out of Richardson's bear-like hands. The boy's rent jacket collar dangled lopsidedly, and his disheveled hair hung in his eyes, which gleamed with satisfaction. He was all but smirking.

"Richardson, let the boy alone. I'll deal with him."

"You'd better." The tall man we believed to be an informer stepped in so close that his fishy breath filled my senses. His face tightened, and he waggled his finger under my nose.

I swatted his hand away. "Keep your distance!"

Richardson stepped back but sneered, "I'd keep a close watch on that boy if I were you." He looked at the two of us, then quickly turned and headed north. Toward General Bridgewater's headquarters, I immediately thought, although other destinations also lay in that direction.

Once the crowd dispersed, I twisted the boy around to face me. "What in tarnation was that about?"

Christopher giggled at my language. "You've never talked like that before."

"You've never exasperated me so much before. What did you do to make Richardson put his hands on you?"

We walked along Fish Street, dodging patches of ice and hard-packed snow. Christopher fiddled with his jacket, trying to make the torn collar look less conspicuous as we neared the tavern.

"Do you think Molly will notice it's ripped?"

"Yes, no way to hide you've been in a scuffle. Again, I'll ask. Will you tell me what you were doing?"

A heavy sigh escaped the boy's chapped lips. "I've been following him, it's true. I didn't know that he saw me though." He looked up and said in earnest, "I really didn't think he saw." He sighed again.

We walked in silence. After a block, he whispered. "He knows I know about the tea."

Two horse-drawn sleighs passed before I responded. "And the general?"

"I s'pose so."

"Yes, Richardson's not one to remain quiet. Not when it concerns his livelihood for sure," I thought aloud.

Christopher sighed once more. "Am I gonna get in trouble?"

I reached out, wrapped my arm around his thin shoulders, and hugged him briefly. "No, but perhaps it's best you stay away for a bit."

"I can do that."

I hoped he would, but wondered if he could.

Molly Weston

Christopher and Geoffrey stood silent as sentinels, backs to the great room's hearth, hands stretched behind to warm them. I turned Christopher's jacket inside out to assess the damage. "This'll need a stitch or two. How did you rip your coat? No, don't tell me. I'd rather not know what kind of mischief you've been into." My eyes, however, bored into Geoffrey's.

"Don't blame me!" He raised his hands in mock surrender. "I'm the one who rescued him from Richardson."

"So you say." Turning to Christopher, I gently placed the jacket in his hands. "Take this into the kitchen. I'll be in shortly to repair it."

Once we were alone, I embraced Geoffrey. I laid my head against his chest, my cheek soaking up the cool from outside. "He's such an adventurous lad, always on the lookout for excitement. I can't stop thinking that he's going to be hurt by all this spying."

"Shh. You're trembling!" Geoffrey whispered as he rubbed my back gently. "He'll be fine. Richardson is more bluster than trouble."

I pulled away to gaze at his face and noticed fine lines of worry around his eyes. *He doesn't believe his own words.* With a sigh, I caressed his face and made my way into the kitchen to mend the torn collar.

Beeswax candles jutted out from the basket I carried over my left arm. I balanced the load while selecting the choicest apples from a wooden barrel. The market teemed with shoppers swarming the street and its stalls, but all the hustle and bustle didn't hide me from Hester Winslow's sharp eyes and caustic personage.

"Molly!" The voice screeched my name. I cringed automatically and dropped an apple. From the corner of my eye, I spotted the fruit vendor rubbing his ear.

In an instant, she was at my side. "Molly! It's been too long. Come and let's have a hot drink to warm us on this cold afternoon." The vicious viper looped her arm through mine, sliding the basket off with her free hand. "I'll help you and carry this bundle."

Somehow, I managed to pay the vendor for the few apples I'd selected, which put me a half step behind her. With a long step and a skip, I caught up to her pace. "Are you doing your own shopping now?"

Hester laughed and patted my forearm. "Don't be silly. I'm out for a stroll. It's good to be out with people, you know."

I did know. Hester frequently promenaded through the city searching for opportunities to be seen with the people who could best help her clamber up the rungs of society. We didn't particularly enjoy spending time together. In fact, socializing with me could lower her standing. An alarm bell rang in my subconscious at her desire to seek out my company, and a now familiar uneasiness returned as we walked toward the coffeehouse.

My unease grew as I sat across the table from her. The color rose in my cheeks as I compared her appearance to mine. Hester's hair, perfectly curled and swept up in a pleasing style, framed blue eyes fringed with long lashes. Feeling a bit disarranged, I quickly replaced errant tresses escaping my close-fitting cap. However, there could be no easy improvement for my rumpled, food-stained clothing dotted with ash. I studied my work-worn hands, noting the red, chapped knuckles and torn nails.

"Molly, would you care for a cup of tea?"

I shoved my hands into my lap. "No. I respect the boycott. No tea."

Hester's head swiveled as she inspected the room and its customers. Her attention returned to me, and she smiled as her voice assumed a beguiling tone. "Oh, come now. Nobody will fault you for taking one cup, especially here."

I sucked in my lips to not explode in anger. "Standing against the Townshend Acts may seem fruitless to you, but these additional taxes hurt everyone. You and Cyrus may afford to pay more, but many of us cannot. When I don't drink tea, I'm letting my neighbors know that I care about them and their future." Insolence crept into my voice. "Tea, and drinking it, may not seem an important issue to you, but it is to me."

Hester's eyes widened, but she made no mention of having heard me. "This tea is delicious with a spoonful of cream." She raised her cup and sipped the steaming liquid.

Resigned to my current state, I sighed. "How have you been keeping, Hester?"

Her lips curled upward at my query, yet she placed her cup on its saucer before replying. "It's always good to keep current with friends, and it's been quite some time since we've had an afternoon chat."

I longed to be elsewhere—any place would be an improvement. My gaze settled beyond her shoulder at the portrait of King George III. The artwork depicted a hunting motif: the white setter's coat spotted black and meticulously combed, a hooded falcon resting on a gloved hand. The silence between us grew as I studied the painting.

Finally, she leaned toward me. "All this talk about tea and boycotts and raids and such. Don't you grow tired thinking about it?"

I gasped aloud, and my eyes snapped back to hers. This woman, always preoccupied with fashion and society, never expressed an interest in politics. Hester always had a scheme in motion, but this uncharacteristic comment provided no clue as to what she was planning.

"No, Hester, not at all. I'm determined to help in any way I can."

"That's why you started the spinning circles?"

Again, she surprised me. That Hester paid heed to our spinning contests focused my thoughts. My inner alarm still rang, and I proceeded cautiously. "Ye-e-es, why do you ask? Surely, you're not interested in spinning with us."

My tea-drinking companion laughed quietly. "No, of course not. But I have been thinking about how I can help Boston women in their efforts."

Had I not been sitting, I'd have fainted to the floor. I closed the distance between us and whispered, "You want to help? Then why are we here in a Loyalist establishment? Why are *you* drinking tea?"

"I'm sure you must find it confusing." She reached across the table and patted my hand. "It's rather simple. I've had a change of heart. But I simply cannot give up my tea."

I sat back in my chair and stared at Hester, listening to the hypocrisy drip from her words as she talked about spinning circles while drinking tea. *If she's had a change of heart, it's because something will benefit her.* "And?"

"What can I do?" Hester spread her fingers and examined them. "Not spinning, of course." Her eyebrows raised as she raised the cup filled with her beverage of choice.

My stomach lurched, and coffee-flavored bile rose in the back of my throat. Snippets of what she might be planning floated in my thoughts, but none of them anchored themselves to a favorable outcome for anyone save her. "Well, I, uh, nothing comes to mind at the moment." I swallowed and forced a smile. "I'm sure we can find a place for you somewhere."

Hester Winslow

In the richly decorated entryway of the general's house, I waited for him to conclude a meeting. On my left, two upholstered Queen Anne chairs graced a round, black walnut table that furnished the small foyer. Above the table hung a still life featuring an abundance of grapes, framed in gilt. A tall porcelain vase, which likely overflowed with flowers in spring and summer, sat empty. Elegance surrounded me, yet I felt as hollow as that vase. With my hand, I traced the intricately carved mahogany panel and admired the woodworker's delicate touch.

For two years now, I have been providing him with detailed information about the mill, but all he's done is fill me with tea and biscuits. I shuddered to remember how Commissioner Burch weaseled his way into spending time with me. To chase that memory from my mind, I quickly turned to study the set of closed doors separating me from the man with the power to lift me into a higher social standing.

Suddenly, the doors flew open, and my mouth and eyes mimicked the motion. Lt. Geoffrey Canfield briskly strode out and into my outstretched hand. "Oh!"

"Pardon me," he said quietly. The lieutenant clasped my elbows to keep me upright and then caught sight of my face. "Mrs. Winslow? What?" He stopped mid-sentence; it was as if he comprehended the reason for me to be in the general's entryway. With a tip of his hat, he stepped around me and through the door.

My throat constricted. I wanted to call out to him, but couldn't think of a legitimate reason to explain my presence. *Could he truly deduce the reason for my being here?* In my mind's eye, a powder keg blew up my future.

"Mrs. Winslow!" the general bellowed. "Are you going to stand there or come in?"

I hesitated, but only briefly, before passing through the doorway. "Yes, of course. Beautiful day, isn't it, General Bridgewater?"

My petticoat caught up with me as I reached the chairs positioned in front of the grand oak desk cluttered with papers. At the upper corner, two quills crossed indelicately on a stack of documents. Nearby, puddles of black surrounded an unstoppered silver inkwell. Behind the desk, small piles of ash and chunks of coal littered the hearth. The slovenliness of the office extended to the man himself.

The general loomed behind the desk, his swollen midsection at eye level. I forced my eyes upward to avoid staring at the buttons struggling to close his red dress coat. A brownish stain peeked from behind the medals hanging from his garment. Dull gray hair in need of a comb fell over his ears and across his collar.

With a quickness belying his size, the British officer slammed his hands on the desk and bent forward. His body covered the entire table as it closed the distance between us, and his eyes narrowed as he silently examined me. "*Why* are you here?"

Briefly, I adjusted my petticoat, brushing out the folds. For the first time, I sensed the disdain he bore for anyone living in America and asked myself the same question. Sitting up a bit straighter, I fixed my eyes on his. "Molly."

"Who? Oh, yes, the barmaid."

"Indeed. I'm making progress, getting closer to her."

"Do you have anything of value to report other than you're *getting close*? You've been *getting close* for some time now."

"Well, no, but it shouldn't be long until I have good news for you."

The general slapped the papers and stood upright. "Don't waste my time till you do!" He turned and faced the fire.

I hesitated a moment, unsure whether I'd been dismissed. "Sir?"

His head turned toward me. "You're still here? What is it now?"

My stomach quivered. "I, uh, I'll send word when I have what you want to hear."

"Hmmph." He glared and then showed me his back once more.

I adjusted the shawl around my shoulders, picked up my purse, sliding its strings over my wrist, and slipped out the door, hoping to escape the insecurity that the last hour deposited in my mind.

Geoffrey Canfield

My nerves, long strained by the general and freshly aggravated from chancing upon that woman at his office, wearied me as I strode through the frozen streets. Eli would want to know that she had visited the general. Molly had relayed her talk over tea with Hester and her concern about the woman's sudden desire to assist the spinning circles. Combined with young Chris's information about the general and the tea house master, my mind couldn't stop circling round the idea that Hester and the general had some plan concerning tea.

With each step, my boots kicked up newly fallen snow. The whiteness swirled around my head, hindering my vision, but it quieted the cadence of soldiers training on the Common and mellowed the discordant sounds of conversation. It muffled the clops of passing horses and squeaky wheels of drays laden with market goods. Frosty powder dusted everything beneath it, softening the hard edges of doorways and windowsills. Only three years ago, I'd have rejoiced in the beautiful silence and basked in its attendant peacefulness. Today, however, the snow brought only stillness and fresh worries.

♥

Eli exploded at hearing of Hester's treachery. "That little snake!" He slammed his fist onto the table in my quarters. "You were right all along. Cotton needs to distract her some more."

I shrugged off my uniform coat and draped it over the bedpost. "How long can this chicanery work? She's not entirely unintelligent."

My friend exploded in scornful laughter. "She's so intent on executing her own schemes, I doubt she's given any thought as to whether she's the one being manipulated. The general is manipulating her as much as she thinks she's manipulating Cotton."

I wasn't as certain as my friend, but then he'd known her for many years. "Where do we find Cotton these days?"

Eli neared the door. "Not sure, but Christopher will know."

Christopher Snider

Eli and Geoffrey think I'm a good spy. They've given me another mission: find Cotton and task him with interfering in Missus Winslow's plans. I've been thinking about this and don't think we need Cotton. If they want him to bungle her plans, well, there's no need to get him to do it. I can botch them good enough.

After walking all over town and visiting with almost every shop owner, I finally saw Missus Winslow go into Crown Coffeehouse. I hid in a doorway before she saw me. 'Twas hard to keep out of sight with no one on the streets. I waited outside till my toes near froze before she came out, and then followed her.

Egad! It was so boring! She went in and out of shops the rest of the afternoon, and I never got a chance to eat or get warm. I was so happy to go back to the tavern for my evening chores and supper, even if my toes and fingers stung like crazy from the cold. Molly gave me some old wool socks to wear on my hands.

Yesterday's spy work tired me out, so today I went to school. Mr. Conrad rapped my knuckles once because I fell asleep during the reading lesson. It hurt real bad. They're still red.

These socks help a lot. My hands were warmer today while I watched Missus Winslow. Tomorrow's market day. No school! Huzzah!

FEBRUARY 22, 1770

Geoffrey Canfield

On the way to Lillie's shop, my mind wandered back to earlier events. It all began with the nonimportation agreement. According to news from Britain, the agreement is producing results as their manufactories are suffering. Boston's citizenry reveled in that news, but the boycott wasn't handing them the complete victory they had desired. Merchants still sell European goods; tea and clothing are still purchased in shops up and down King Street, even if their owners signed the agreement. In many respects, commerce in Boston has continued despite Molly's efforts to convince merchants to participate in the boycott. Purchasers simply know where to go to fulfill their desires.

Even so, we did experience several demonstrations. As we patrolled to keep the peace, we commonly saw crowds taunting and jeering the non-signing shopkeepers as they opened their establishments. More frequently, protestors took out their frustrations on them. Up and down the street, freshly lettered "Don't Buy from this Traitor" slogans overlaid the proprietors' names.

On the eighth of the month, demonstrators confronted merchants who refused to cooperate. As shoppers weaved through the boisterous crowd to enter and exit shops, I feared for the safety of the townswomen doing their marketing as well as that of the merchants. Five days ago, the crowds traded words for actions, and the roughest of the lot threw stones at merchants, broke windows, and defaced shop signs. Especially designated for ill treatment were Messrs. Lillie, Taylor, Rogers, Bernard, and McMasters. The crowd didn't exclude women from their wrath, and the shop of sisters Ame and Elizabet Cummings, milliners by trade, suffered the same treatment. The Body of the People found all guilty of violating the boycott, and for a week, effigies of these merchants danced before their doors.

Today, Thursday, is market day. Farmers from outlying areas bring in their crops, hoping to entice housewives and cooks who poke, squeeze, and smell before making their purchase. Streets teem with dray wagons, drawn by horses or yoked oxen and filled with produce or other wares. The requisite pigs, sheep, and occasional milk cow roam the streets before being corralled. To be heard above the bleats and squeals, hagglers shout. And in the midst of the benevolent chaos are the schoolboys. Schools close on market days, leaving youth of all ages with a day free of cares. Today, tens and tens of these fellows celebrated their freedom by gathering in front of Lillie's house.

General Bridgewater learned of another growing mob and ordered my patrol to keep the peace, so we headed into the North End. By the time we arrived at three o'clock, any truce was heading out to sea. Dancing in the freezing temperature was a four-faced figure jammed onto a long pole. Its bearer surprised me—Christopher Snider. The makeshift totem rose above the throng of boys bundled in woolen coats. Some wore scarves wrapped around their necks and heads to keep out the cold wind blowing inland. The icy air did nothing to cool their enthusiastic shrieks of approval as the effigy passed by.

Their cries grew louder, drawing the buyers' attention.

"Scoundrel!"

"Sign or starve!"

"You're all traitors!"

The crowd's frenetic energy multiplied as men and women left the market and made their way to Lillie's. Deeper voices joined the young tenors, and the shouts turned contemptuous as old and young members of the Body harassed Lillie.

"Freedom from tyranny!"

Worried that the crowd would grow violent, I ordered my men to break ranks and mingle with the masses to calm their anger.

"Separate and Disperse!"

Lillie, standing at the doorway to his home, looked increasingly vulnerable to the growing dissension. Sensing the need to protect him from the rabble-rousers, I began to make my way toward him. The crowd was thick as mud in a bog and just as difficult to wade through. I advanced slowly, making more progress sidestepping to the right, then the left, rather than forging a direct path. As I neared the front of the crowd, someone jostled me from behind, knocking me into an angry protester. I sorted myself from the ruffian, and a quick flash of movement drew my eye. Ebenezer Richardson jumped up to knock the carved head off the pole. His actions didn't surprise me. Richardson worked at the Customs House, and many Sons of Liberty spoke of him as the informer responsible for the warehouse raids. I knew that I needed to turn my attentions to the young fellow.

Christopher was an able opponent despite his small size. Twice more Richardson jumped, and twice the lad swung the pole away from the man's reach. Fearing that Richardson would injure the boy, I moved to intercept the provocateur. Before I could reach the adversaries, harsh shouts rang out as the rabble surrounded the eldest.

"Traitor!"

"Informer!"

Richardson broke through the mob and ran for his house, but not before stopping to argue with Edward Proctor and Thomas Knox. More shouts pierced the crowd's commotion.

"Perjury! It's perjury!" he bellowed and ran through his front door.

As if a school of fish, the crowd swiveled and swam toward Richardson's house. I feared they meant to do him harm, but my men and I, now scattered throughout the crowd, were in no position to render assistance. All we could do was watch events unfold.

The protestors split into groups and surrounded the house. Christopher and his friends continued to harass Lillie, creating a human chain as they paraded their grotesque effigy in circles. George Wilmot, a seaman and friend of Richardson, threaded his way through the crowd.

"Let me in," he pleaded.

"Best to not interfere," I answered.

"He's my friend. I can help cool his temper."

I nodded and let him pass.

Richardson next appeared when he flung open a second-floor window, yelling to the crowd below.

"By the eternal God, I will make it too hot for some of you before tonight!"[9]

In response, the crowd roared and pelted his house with rocks and brickbats. Broken clumps of brick smashed windows, demolishing glass, wooden sashes, and leaded mullions. Not everyone possessed an archer's aim, and consequently, a few rioters suffered the landings of errant missiles on their own skulls. Bloodied and in pain, the mob carried on, swimming in an eddy of hysteria.

"Calm yourselves!" I cried. "Halt!"

My commands went unheeded, and in fact, I doubted they were even heard over the din. I regretted my earlier command to separate my patrol. We needed a combined force to make our presence known, felt, and obeyed. I hoped that Wilmot would succeed in calming Richardson because my singular efforts to pacify the mob were failing.

Shouts and rocks filled the air till a shot pierced the racket. An immediate silence, as quiet as the din was loud, fell over the square. Then, more shots, screams, and shrieks, higher-pitched than before, saturated the stillness. To save their own hides, some of the riotous cowards began to flee, yet three men knelt on the ground. Quickly, a few more stopped running and stood sentry—pushing and shoving away angry rioters. 'Twas a valiant effort to keep the crowd from trampling those kneeling. Believing that someone had been hurt, or worse, I elbowed my way upstream through the escaping crowd to reach the trio on the ground.

♥

My heart tore. A young boy, who from his size I judged couldn't have been more than ten or eleven years old, lay on the street, the life draining from his shattered body and congealing on the frozen ground. When I drew nearer, I saw his face and recognized him from his time at The Three Lions.

"It's young Christopher," one of the men said softly.

"Was Ebenezer who shot him," said a second.

"Lift him," I commanded. "We need to get the sheriff and locate the boy's parents. You!" I pointed to the nearest man. "Go find Dr. Warren."

While the men gently lifted Christopher and carried him to a nearby house, several in the mob, armed with muskets and cutlasses, broke into Richardson's dwelling. I signaled to a few members of my squad to join me, but before we could enter, the gang exited, dragging Richardson and Wilmot by force.

"Unhand them," I commanded.

My men pulled the criminals away from the agitators. Positioning two soldiers in front and two behind, we left to find a justice. With sharpened bayonets pointed at their backs, Richardson and Wilmot cooperated, entrusting us with their lives. The mob followed, waving nooses and threatening immediate death to the villains. Thankfully, William Molineux worked through the crowd to keep the most outrageous tempers at bay.

Justice of the Peace John Ruddock ordered us to Faneuil Hall. By the time we reached that edifice, our audience had grown. I'd never seen such a large crowd as the one occupying the hall that evening. Nearly a thousand people attended the interview conducted by Justices of the Peace Richard Dana, Samuel Pemberton, and Edmund Quincy. After the examination, the justices ordered Richardson and Wilmot to the city gaol.

We accompanied the criminals once again as we marched through the city. Halters and nooses plagued us on all sides, but we safely ensconced them with nary a rope burn.

Young Christopher, however, didn't fare as well as his murderers. Although attended by Dr. Warren, the boy lost his life several hours after being shot. News of his death spread faster than fire in a haystack that night. William Molineux and fellow Sons of Liberty worked overtime to calm the crowd to great success, or else Richardson would have hung within hours for his wicked deed.

February 23–28, 1770

Molly Weston

On the Death of Mr. Snider, Murder'd by Richardson

In heaven's eternal court it was decreed
How the first martyr for the cause should bleed
To clear the country of the hated brood
We whet his courage for the common good[10]

Tears flowed as I reread the words of Phillis Wheatley on the freshly printed leaflet. This young slave girl, whose education and resulting literary prose flourished under the watchful eyes of her owners, John and Susanna Wheatley, perfectly captured my feelings in her poem. I hunched over the kitchen table, and soon my shoulders shook, and my chest heaved as sobs broke free from my soul. I cried for the loss of Christopher's life and the grief his parents were suffering, but mostly I cried for myself. I couldn't imagine not seeing him play with Boots and Buttermilk any longer.

In between my sobs, I heard shuffling and soon felt a nudge in my ribs. Boots jumped onto the bench, and his cold, wet nose nuzzled my ear. I reached around his neck and pulled him close. Boots, too, would miss young Chris. I stretched both arms around his neck's soft fur and buried my face in his coat smelling of wood smoke.

"Molly? Molly?"

The voice grew insistent. I sniffed and lifted my head. Geoffrey entered the kitchen and knit his brow when he saw me hugging the dog.

"Christopher?" He slowly drew the leaflet from my fingertips. As he read the ode to Christopher, tears welled up in his eyes.

As he read, I remembered how the little ragamuffin became a fixture at our tavern. He drank in the attention Mother and I poured on him, and he thrived. The child beamed whenever Paul praised his work. And now, a Tory musket has silenced his precocious antics. I ran my hand through Boots's fur to comfort me.

♥

"Hurry, Molly. We mustn't be late."

I flew down the stairs, shrugging on the mantua as I descended. Mother waited in the great room, and as soon as I landed, she headed for the door. "Hurry!"

We kept up a brisk pace to the courthouse. Today was the day of reckoning for the man responsible for Christopher's death, and we both wanted to be present at the inquest. However, the rest of the city felt the same, as did most of the Massachusetts Bay Colony. People coursed through the streets, gathering in front of the government building. From its steps, we looked out and saw individuals grouped on the sidewalks, meeting up with friends to gossip.

When the deputy unlocked the doors, people flowed into the courtroom. Mother and I squeezed in between two portly, gentle-women on the last bench.

We all stood when Peter Oliver, slated to oversee the inquest, entered the room and positioned himself behind the bench. Then entered Boston's selectmen: Joshua Henshaw, Joseph Jackson, John Ruddock, John Hancock, Samuel Pemberton, Henderson Inches, and Jonathan Mason. They filed into the courtroom and lined up in front of the judge's bench. Henshaw carried a lottery box.

Justice Oliver peered down at John Hancock, who didn't break his stare as he stepped forward. I squeezed Mother's arm. "He doesn't look pleased."

Hancock turned and addressed the audience. "Mr. Mason will draw twelve names from the box to serve as members of the jury. When your name is called, please come forward."

Mason and Henshaw stood to join him. He and Henshaw held the box above Mason's eye level. Mason reached into the box for the first name.

"Elijah Smith!"

Mother and I looked around to see where Elijah was seated. We found the short, rotund man in the second row. He rose to join the men at the front of the room.

"Jedediah Williams!"

Heads swiveled right and left, and then whole torsos rotated to take in the entire room, but nobody stood.

Men standing in the back began calling outside the building. "Jedediah Williams!"

"He's coming!" a faceless voice shouted. After a few moments, a man rushed up the aisle, shedding his unkempt winter coat as he approached the queue.

"Abraham Crocker!"

"I object." John Ruddock, one of the selectmen, leaned over and picked the name from Mason's hand. A few people whispered to one another, but Mason drew another name.

"Horatio Kitts!"

"I object," said John Hancock. The murmurs grew louder when he took the name from Mason.

Everyone's head snapped to the bench when Judge Oliver banged the gavel. "For what reason? All the men's names in the box are viable candidates. Not a single name should be rejected."

"It is a selectman's decision to deny a seat on the jury to anyone not deemed suitable for the task," Hancock replied.

Oliver had to accept that answer, but the pink tinge in his cheeks belied his feelings.

Mason drew again. "Solomon Matthews!"

"I object," said Hancock once again.

This time, the judge didn't accept that answer. "This is nonsense! You must have a reason. Matthews is a taxpaying citizen of the colony. He *is* eligible."

Hancock looked in his direction, but his eyes were unfocused, giving him an imperious air. "Matthews is unreliable." He turned to Mason. "Choose another name."

Crimson splotches on the judge's neck grew larger and engulfed his entire face while listening to Hancock and enduring the dismissive attitude shown him. He stared at Hancock, who went about the selectmen's business, ignoring the frosty glare cast his way.

Eventually, the selectmen approved twelve jurors, none of whom lived in Boston proper, and the judge convened the inquest.

After a long day of testimony regarding Ebenezer Richardson, the judge called a recess, but nobody wanted to leave the courthouse. Spectators loitered on the steps and on the walkway in front of the building. We threaded our way through the crowds and paused from time to time to chat with small groups, offering our opinions on the inquest and comparing local gossip that had circulated for days.

"Richardson's got to be guilty."

"I saw him aim the gun at the crowd."

"What was he thinking, shooting at a young boy?"

As darkness settled in, we dispersed. Mother and I headed for The Three Lions and a busy evening of serving suppers and making tomorrow's meal. We planned to attend every day of the inquest, no matter its length.

♥

On Monday, following the shooting, a long article in the *Boston Gazette* spoke of young Christopher's demise and the inquest, vividly portraying the cruelty of Richardson's actions upon the boy's body, in which:

> were found 11 shot or slugs, about the bigness of large peas, one of which pierced his breast about an inch and half above the midriff, and passing clear thro' the right lobe of the lungs, lodged in his back. This, three of the Surgeons, deposed before the Jury of Inquest, was the cause of his death; on which they brought in their verdict, wilful murder by said Richardson. The right hand of the Boy was also cruelly torn, whence it seems to have been across his breast, and to have deadned the force of the shot, which might otherwise have pierced the stomach.[11]

I laid the article on the bedside table and dabbed at my eyes once more before going downstairs. They were wet more than dry since Christopher's death. The little scamp had worked with us for only a year, but he had endeared himself to us.

Mother and I left the tavern shortly after four-thirty and hurried along Fish Street to meet up with the funeral procession. The bereaved gathered at Liberty Tree on Essex Street. As we passed the tree, Mother pointed out a placard nailed to its trunk. Someone, surely a Son of Liberty, had painted these sentiments: "Thou shalt take no Satisfaction for the Life of a MURDERER. He shall surely be put to Death. Though Hand join in Hand, the Wicked shall not pass unpunished. The memory of the just is Blessed."[12]

The Trinity Church bell struck five o'clock, and the pallbearers claimed their positions alongside the casket. The six boys looked to be as young as Christopher. *I didn't even know he had friends outside of the tavern.*

Although I couldn't be sure, it looked as if five hundred schoolboys marched from the Liberty Tree. Thousands of Boston's citizens trailed them. Many of the mourners were women, yet men and children from all parts of the city joined the cortege. Following the last of the sorrowful crowd were Christopher's casket, its youthful pallbearers, and the Snider family. Mother and I fell into step beside the Sniders.

Those who didn't join the procession lined the sidewalks and somberly watched it pass. Children stood on wagons to get a better view, and people hung out of second- and third-story windows to pay their respects. Although the atmosphere was subdued, a few women keened, and others cried silently, but all of us felt the gravity of the child's deathpassing. I hugged my shawl tightly, partly to keep warm, but also to console myself. As we walked, the slow pace, combined with the frigid afternoon air, helped to clear my head. My own grief mellowed as I sensed the common bond of thousands intent on honoring young Chris. *It feels as if everyone in Boston is here. Could Chris's death sway all these people to support the American cause resolutely?*

MARCH 2, 1770

ELI WESTON

The near riot at Lillie's shop in February ended in death, yet that dire circumstance didn't quell the unrest in Boston. Just days after Christopher's funeral and interment, Paul took me aside.

"Cotton's sent word to get down to the ropewalk—they're being overrun by lobsterbalks!"

"What would they want down at Gray's Other than jobs," I muttered. "Still, if Cotton's worried, we'd better move quickly."

Worried that tempers were rising at the ropewalk, we ran toward Gray's. The news didn't surprise me. Once in port, British sailors, experienced at making and repairing ropes and rigging, swarmed Boston's maritime businesses and displaced American men. That Cotton had found a job there was sheer luck.

Intending to calm tempers and avoid violence and possible bloodshed, Paul and I headed over to John Gray's ropewalk between Hutchinson and Atkinson Streets. We could hear the shouts from Milk Street, a block from the building—ropemakers and redcoats were already brawling.

We heard fists smacking faces as we rounded the corner, but our first glance at the ruckus showed many ropeworkers armed with clubs. The large paws of Crispus Attucks, recently returned from The Bahamas, landed blows more frequently than naught. The African towered over most of the men, so his large paws, aided by gravity, rendered several men senseless. Morning sunlight glinted off cutlasses as their owners parried and thrusted. Blood dripped from cuts and gashes, soaking linen and woolen garments and then pooling on the floor.

Cotton stood half a head above many of his coworkers, and we elbowed our way to him. In front of him stood a soldier from the 29th Regiment of Foot, tall enough to look my friend in the eye.

My friend's face, tightly pinched and cheeks pinked, bounced slightly on his feet. I recognized the signs; Cotton was itching to fight. Approaching him from behind, I lightly placed my left hand on his shoulder while gently grasping his closer arm with my right so he couldn't turn and jab me. Paul approached the redcoat, arms raised in a gesture of peace.

"Let's quiet down. We can all remain calm."

The redcoat lowered his weapon, and I felt Cotton's body relax as he exhaled. I tugged at his arm and stepped back. He followed; the redcoat reciprocated by turning aside and separating a few of his men from their combatants. In the end, ropeworkers and soldiers went their own way. Paul, Cotton, and I retreated to the Green Dragon.

"What started the fight?" I asked. "Did you ever find out why the soldiers swarmed the ropewalk?"

Cotton gazed at the tankard in his hands before speaking. "I'm not quite sure how it all began. We were busyworking when the redcoats came in. I was too far away to hear all they said, but I saw Crispus shouting and waving his arms at one of them. Their voices grew louder, and quickly so. Everyone tensed, and I feared another shooting. That's why I sent word."

"Good thing," Paul said, "we arrived before things got too unruly."

Cotton barked in laughter at the idea that the melee was only a minor scuffle and then sighed. I'd seen my friend dejected, but it was because of love. This emotion was similar, and yet different.

He continued. "After I sent the boy, I heard talk of a Sergeant Chambers, who's gone missing. Seems they thought we killed the poltroon. Then, quick as a bolt of lightning, they started pushing and shoving the workers."

"And the workers struck back, and with spirit," I finished.

"Aye. We used whatever was handy, but in the end, it seemed those ruffians wanted only to use their muskets and bayonets on us. Fighting was the only way to stay alive."

"Bad business for everyone," said Paul, "but it seems these redcoats keep provoking us. After Chris's death, they'd do better if they held back."

Cotton looked at me, his eyes slightly squinting. "Surely, you've sensed the same feelings on the wharf, Eli. And Paul, certainly you've heard men speak out. Boston won't abide these soldiers much longer.

Especially after Christopher's death. Richardson may have fired the shot, but we all know who he worked for."

The three of us fell quiet and drank in silence. I don't know what Cotton and Paul were thinking, but as for me, I felt dark forces surrounding us. Little Christopher was right to be worried about the corner preacher's curses; what Geoffrey and I had scoffed at was unfolding before our eyes.

Geoffrey Canfield

"Eli, the Customhouse has taken umbrage with the *Gazette*."

"I'm not surprised, considering that both Edes and Gill are publishing information that shows the commissioners in a poor light."

"Not the commissioners per se, but the claim that Richardson is not and never was an under-officer of the Customs. The commissioners are insisting that the Gazette correct what they published."

"Richardson's not the informer? Ha! Paxton himself has had dealings with Richardson for years. Say, wasn't he Richardson's bondsman in that business a few years ago?"

"He was. But remember that Richardson swore to the grand jury that Paxton had paid him for his part in those riots. Now Paxton's claiming to have had no dealings with Richardson at all."

"Oh, I'm sure that Ben will reveal all of this. He's rather clever at exposing these devious intricacies."[13]

Molly Weston

Eli and Paul dragged their exhaustion into the kitchen shortly after dusk. Though their heads were bent, I could see blood had splattered their coats and painted their faces.

Mother rushed around the kitchen gathering a bowl of warm water, rags, and bandages. I hurriedly filled trenchers with hot stew, searching out the biggest pieces of pork to fill their bellies before fetching mugs of steaming coffee.

In between spoonfuls, Eli related details of the fracas, and Mother daubed at his wounds.

"Ouch!"

"If you'd stop looking for trouble, I wouldn't have to do this." Mother looked sternly at my brother while cleansing a cut on his temple. "For two years now, wherever the riots are is where we find you… always right in the middle of the trouble."

"Did you ever find out why the soldiers were there? They've never interfered with a meeting of the Body before."

Eli's mouth was full, so Paul answered me.

"Nobody really had a reason, but I think it all goes back to the day Chris was shot. Tempers are short all around, and the British think that if they keep us from forming large groups, nobody will conspire against them."

"Hard to imagine why we'd conspire against them." Sarcasm laced Eli's remark. "Richardson's found guilty of killing Chris, yet they can't determine whether he's guilty of informing for the Crown."

"Doesn't really matter now, does it?" I replied. "The verdict ensures he can't tattle any longer."

"It still grates against my sense of justice."

"Of course, it does," Geoffrey interjected. He strode into the kitchen and directly to the coffeepot before joining us at the table. He'd suffered a few injuries as well. A purplish bruise colored his left cheek, and bloodied scabs gilded his knuckles.

"Bridgewater's apprehensive, nervous," he began, "about losing control in the city. For Boston, they lost a young boy to an informant.

For the general, he lost a source of personal revenue and gained a lot of ill will from the constituents."

"What's his next move?" Paul asked.

Geoffrey stroked his chin before answering. "I'm not sure. He wasn't pleased with today's events, but he can be wily. I think it's important for all of us to proceed calmly. Paul, use the time you spend with the tavern customers to track conversations."

"You want me to spy on our customers? They're all patriots."

"No, no, not like that. It's important to learn how they're feeling, if they are quieting."

"Because if they aren't, Bridgewater will intervene with force?" Eli asked.

"Not necessarily, but it wouldn't be unusual for him to request additional troops from Howe."

"That would take months," I said, "and it would agitate everyone all the more. Even the general would know that an increase in animosity isn't a good thing."

Geoffrey sighed and rubbed his eyes. "The city needs to remain calm. There won't be any peace if Americans continue to inflame their emotions."

I popped to my feet, suddenly feeling as if my beloved had placed all the blame for the riotous behavior on me. "We aren't the only ones involved! Those redcoats harass us whenever they can. You've seen them torment dock workers at the wharf, and how many times have women been accosted by British soldiers and sailors? We can't even walk after sunset without looking behind us every few steps."

I closed the distance between us and admonished him with a finger. "How many soldiers have been caught or punished for their behavior?"

"Molly, no!" Geoffrey's eyes grew wide at my outburst; Eli and Paul stopped chewing. Mother circled the table to put her arms around me. She patted my back.

"Shh, Molly. Geoffrey isn't implying that only Americans are causing problems. You're overly emotional because you're still mourning Christopher, but you need to see things as they truly are."

All at once, I felt foolish and lowered my gaze rather than looking at the men. Composing myself, I crossed the room and, without saying a word, grasped Geoffrey's cup. To apologize, I refilled it and brought him a coriander cooky.

He graciously accepted my humble peace offering. "Many soldiers are easily excitable these days. Being away from their country and continually surrounded by people who don't want them wears on their emotions. Plus, not all of us are so eager to fight." A smile and a wink sealed his words.

♥

Once Eli, Paul, and Mother retired for the evening, Geoffrey and I huddled close to the hearth for warmth. Although I would never admit it to anyone, I hoped for something more. The fire's dying embers flared as he poked at the coals, and a wave of heat toasted our legs. As he leaned back, I squeezed his hand.

"You must understand something, Molly." He patted the hand that gripped his. "These British soldiers, the ones who prey on the vulnerable."

"You mean women?"

He smiled and looked beyond my shoulder. "Yes, you women, but also the others who are overlooked."

"Christopher?"

"And others. Their emotions are being tried, just as ours are. But you must know that I will always side with you. Regardless of the consequences I may suffer, my allegiance is with you, your family and friends."

He leaned in to kiss me, but I caressed his cheeks and pulled back to study his expression. Geoffrey raised his eyebrows as if to question my action, but before he could utter a sound, I covered his lips with mine.

Outside the tavern's kitchen, a gust of wind rattled the windowpanes and swirled the snowflakes as they started to fall.

MARCH 5, 1770

Eli Weston

Paul replenished tankards as fast as Molly collected them. Customers started to drift in about four o'clock, but none had left. As dusk fell, the clientele of The Three Lions swelled with men, young and old, railing at the British who had invaded the ropewalk in search of their missing sergeant. Some wore their bruises and scrapes like badges of honor. Others falsely boasted of magnificent feats of boxing, to the guffaws of everyone. All conversation centered around the ropewalk melee. Several hours later, the great room had become a standing room, all benches occupied and only a few empty places to stand.

"Those British thingumbobs have no right to blame us for their sergeant gone missin'."

"Heard he was out being pleasured, if you know what I mean."

"And why do they get a chance at jobs that are rightfully ours? They're just a bunch of corny-faced jackanapes wanting to fatten their purses."

"Let the Royal Navy pay 'em."

This last comment blasted out of the seaman Crispus Attucks. After returning from his last voyage, he'd been looking for a place to trade his skills for a wage. Several days earlier, we'd seen him trade blows with a few sailors at the Gray's ropewalk.

The passion infected me, and I couldn't keep quiet any longer. "Ha! How much do you think those sailors are paid? Why do you think the Crown keeps raising our taxes? To pay them more!"

Attucks's ire and voice flamed in response. "The Englanders are earning twice—once through our jobs and again through our taxes."

"Huzzah! Huzzah!" The crowd cheered.

"Meanwhile, we twiddle our thumbs as the bull calves frolic." A tall man, Attucks knew how to use his height to advantage, and he towered over his seated listeners as he weaved through the benches. He looked like a preacher lecturing his congregants about eternal damnation on a Sunday morning.

Attucks pounded his chest and then waved his hand to encompass all the men. "We'll calm down when our jobs return to us." Boisterous congregants slammed their tankards on the tables, beating a rhythm in support of the speaker.

Suddenly, many in the drunken crowd stood and roared, pointing at the door to my back.

I turned to see a British sailor shutting the door.

Attucks's voice boomed over the hysteria. "Look who dares to drink with us! He takes our jobs and then expects us to quench his thirst!"

The dark giant pushed his way back to his table, and then his head dipped below the crowd. For a moment, I thought he'd retaken his seat, but then he stood, a Goliath among men, a club in each hand.

The sailor's face paled, and he took two steps back.

Fearing a confrontation, I shouted, "Attucks! Not here!"

The sailor ducked out the door.

Attucks stared at the now-empty space a while longer and then silently crossed the threshold into the night. Nearly half the crowd followed him.

Paul, tugging at my elbow, forced my eyes away from the exiting drunks. "We should go, too, Eli. I have a bad feeling about this. Crispus has been in a bad way since Friday's fight. Maybe we can intercept him."

♥

"Cotton's right about that."

"What's that?" Paul asked.

"Ha! Didn't realize I was talking out loud." My brother and I walked briskly along Fish Street toward Dock Square, following Crispus and his supporters. We kept our heads down as we faced the glacial wind. "Was thinking about how tired people are of being watched over… "

Shouts interrupted our conversation. We ran the last block to where a crowd had gathered in Dock Square, next to Faneuil Hall and the Customs House. Dozens of people stood face-to-face with redcoats in Boylston's Alley.

Edward Archbald and William Merchant stood facing a soldier, striking a broadsword against the brick wall; sparks flew from the hits. A mean-looking fellow, armed with a large cudgel, stood next to him. The soldier turned and struck Edward on the arm, then pushed William with the sword, ripping his coat.

William returned the blow with a stick, and the cudgel-wielding brute ran into the soldier barracks. He returned with two soldiers, who immediately pursued William, beating him over the head.

Before long, church bells rang in the distance. A second bell quickly answered. In response, more people raced to the square already teeming with people bundled against the biting wind. My nerves jangled when I recognized certain individuals in the crowd who possessed a violent nature. The first I saw was Robert Paterson, one of the more raucous of the rabble in front of Lillie's shop. Behind him was Nathaniel Fosdick, a ropemaker involved in the fracas with Cotton a few days back. I also noticed a few seafaring Americans aligned with the citizens. Kit Monk, a shipwright's apprentice, carried a hammer. Right in front of them all stood Crispus Attucks, still holding those two clubs.[14]

I scanned the crowd for Geoffrey, hoping we could rely on his steady hand and authority to calm the troops. I didn't see my friend wasn't among the other soldiers from the 29th Regiment standing guard at the Customs House. Those British faces stared straight ahead at the angry mob—I could almost see them swallow the fear roiling in their bellies.

"Hey!"

Paul, standing slightly behind, suddenly fell into me, forcing me into the fellow on the other side, and so on. We tumbled like dominoes, the last man bumping up against a redcoat. The soldier, holding his rifle in two hands, stepped out of line and pushed back. More soldiers followed his lead, and soon redcoats punched and pushed as much as we gave.

From the corner of my eye, I saw Paterson wildly swinging at anyone within arm's reach. A few feet away, Monk brandished his hammer like a sword, blindly waving it back and forth, striking soldiers and citizens alike. Blood flowed from gashed foreheads, cheeks, and ears. Scarves, kerchiefs, hats—all soaked up the red.

"Get to Monk," I ordered Paul, "or at least get that hammer!"

Paul threaded his way through the combatants to reach the apprentice. I left to find Paterson, but quickly felt another push, this one from behind. Twisting right, I spotted a raised rifle aimed at my chest. I ducked below the six-foot firearm and dived for the soldier. The blow hit him below the waist, and he flew over my back, landing on the brick pavement. Still in a crouch, I pivoted and snatched the rifle from his limp grip.

A boyish visage, eyes wide with fear, looked up at me. I set the weapon aside and offered my hand for assistance. Hesitantly, he reached up and grasped it. Once he was afoot, I thrust the rifle into his hands and pushed him out of the melee.

"Find Lieutenant Canfield. Hurry!"

Geoffrey Canfield

The 29th Regiment of Foot was on guard at the Customs House. My eight-man patrol was returning to the barracks when we came upon Edward Garrick and a group of young men.

The wigmaker's apprentice, drunk on rum, began throwing snowballs at Captain Lieutenant John Goldfinch.

"Go back to England, redcoat!"

Other young men followed suit, hurling snowballs at the guard. Despite the barrage, to his credit, Goldfinch held his ground.

Garrick then recognized the soldier from the wigmaking shop, where he had made a purchase earlier.

"You take our jobs but don't pay your debts! You swindle our merchants. Do you pay for anything?" "You bloody back!" With each insult, Garrick launched an icy projectile.

Before I could intervene, Hugh White, another soldier from the regiment, rushed to Goldfinch's defense, yelling, "Hold your tongue, rogue! You don't know what you're talking about!"

Garrick responded by poking White, who, as quick as a fox, whacked him on the head with the butt of his musket. A few boys surrounded the bleeding Garrick, while older youth packed snow around rocks and continued to pelt White and Goldfinch with the more dangerous ammunition.

Fire bells began ringing, and the square filled with people, packing the area in front of the Customs House steps. Towering above the growing mob, I espied Crispus Attucks, facing the soldiers, who now held their muskets in a protective stance. Unfortunately, the aggressive posture didn't deter the group, which came armed with sticks.

The group began jeering, and one stepped forward to swat at a musket with his stick. Others immediately joined in, forming a line and striking each musket as they passed by.[15]

I looked for Captain Preston in the nearby barracks, and he joined us outside.

Eli Weston

Paul and I fell back from the front line of agitators just as John Hicks knocked a soldier to the ground. He stood up, but the boys surged forward, driving the soldiers into the barracks. Shortly thereafter, more soldiers emerged, this time bearing cutlasses, clubs, and bayonets, and they set out to harm the boys.

Captain Preston emerged with a party of soldiers, bayonets affixed to their muskets. They pushed through the crowds, bayonets forward.

"Make way! Make way!" they cried, as they braved the barrage of snowballs.

Someone, perhaps Captain Preston, shouted, "Fire! Damn you, fire! Be the consequence what it will!"

In response, a soldier fired, but a protester promptly struck his hands with his cudgel. The soldier dropped his weapon.

That first shot, however, introduced a flurry of balls into the crowd.

Shouts, screams, blood, and the fog of spent powder filled the square.

Molly Weston

Mother and I chatted while we washed tankards, trenchers, and spoons, so we didn't notice the quiet right away.

"Molly. Shh!" Mother rested her finger on her lips and then lightly tapped her ear.

I turned toward the great room, and then I sensed the absence of noise. Gently, I pressed the door open, enough for a peek at empty seats and tables cluttered with tankards. A few customers still in their cups remained scattered throughout the room. The tavern was never this quiet at nine o'clock.

I grabbed my mantua.

"Where are you going?"

"Mother, something doesn't feel right. I have to find Eli and Paul."

"And Geoffrey?"

"And Geoffrey."

Shortly after turning onto Fish Street, I heard the alarm bells. I quickened my pace and soon heard the riotous commotion. Fear gripped my heart, and I began to run toward the disturbance.

CRACK!

Gunfire!

CRACK! CRACK! CRACK!

I reached the edge of the mob as the final shot was fired. Frantic, I searched the crowd for my brothers. I moved forward as people began to disperse, continuing my search. My mind envisioned horrible images of them lying in the street, which grew stronger as I came across Samuel Gray. I gagged when I saw that a large portion of his skull was missing. The second victim had been in the tavern only an hour earlier. Crispus Attucks lay on his back, with two balls in his breast.

Seeing Crispus intensified my fear, and I called out. "Eli! Paul! Where are you?"

Soldiers, no longer firing, continued to harass the townspeople's efforts to reach the wounded.

"Stay back!" One pushed me into the man standing beside me. Angry, I pushed back, but the man quickly grabbed me.

"Don't make yourself a victim!"

I shook myself loose and continued searching. The shouting had quieted, now replaced with moans from the wounded and cries from the bystanders. I nearly stumbled over Samuel Maverick and Christopher Monk, both seventeen years old, and then came upon James Caldwell. I stooped to see whether I could administer aid to him as he lay face down on the street. But he was dead.

Tears fell from my eyes at the scene. To my right lay John Clark, and to my left, Edward Payne held his arm tightly to stem the flow of blood. Beyond him, John Green, Robert Paterson, Patrick Carr, and David Parker—all bleeding profusely. Finally, my eyes found Eli, with Paul kneeling beside him.

GEOFFREY CANFIELD

The atmosphere was tense, but manageable until Captain Preston yelled, "Hold your fire!" A soldier, having his musket hammered by a youth, regained control of his gun and fired. At that point, chaos erupted. Soldier after soldier fired into the crowd. I counted eleven shots, but more balls could have flown.

People screamed and shouted. Townspeople fought with fists against soldiers with bayonets. The far edges of the mob began to disperse, and I wrangled my men, who were interfering with those giving aid to the wounded.

Then I saw Molly kneeling in the muddy street. Next to my friend, Eli.

Paul was by her side, and I quickly approached them, shoving bystanders to clear my path.

"Grab his shoulders, Paul," I ordered. With Molly still holding Eli's wound closed, I positioned myself between his thighs. "We lift on three. One, two, three." We heaved the man upward and began the sojourn back to The Three Lions.

The following afternoon, after handing in my report on the event to General Bridgewater, I joined the Westons in the kitchen.

Molly Weston

Mother and I looked after Eli as best we could. We laid him on the kitchen table, where we would have plenty of room to work. Drs. Young and Warren, tending to the wounded, promised to come as soon as possible. I gathered clean water and rags as Mother stripped off his upper clothes. As we began to clean the wound, we realized it wasn't as dire as I first thought. The ball had entered just under his right armpit and exited without damaging any bone. So we washed and bandaged him and kept vigil, watching for any sign of fever and infection.

I awoke to a gentle shake. Rubbing my eyes, I realized it was morning, and Father was standing over me.

"I see you nodded off. How's Eli?"

I laid my hand across his forehead and peered closely at his face. No beads of perspiration, a strong indication of pain, were visible. His forehead was cool, no sign of fever. "I find it hard to believe, but he's doing well."

"In the war, how often men would heal from wounds depended on their strength and health before being shot. Eli stands a good chance of being up and about soon."

The kitchen door opened, and Dr. Warren entered, carrying his medical satchel. Pale skin and bloodshot eyes revealed his exhaustion.

"You're correct, Jonathan. Now, let me examine him so I can validate your prognosis."

♥

We haven't heard from Geoffrey since he left last night. He had deposited Eli on the table and headed back to the square, so I was surprised when he reentered the kitchen later that afternoon.

"Molly, we have to talk."

I looked around the kitchen. Mother and Father were present, as was Paul. Dr. Warren had redressed Eli's wound, but Mother was plying him with biscuits and coffee.

"Here?"

"It makes no difference. We are with friends, and I hope, soon to be family."

Family?

"Molly, after last night, I fear the situation here in Boston will worsen. And I no longer wish to wait. It will be difficult, and we may face danger. But I have to ask. Will you stand by my side and marry me?"

My knees began to shake, and he quickly grasped my elbows to steady me. From the corner of my eye, I saw Mother and Father smile.

"Yes."

If you've enjoyed reading *Revolutionary Spark,* be sure to tell your friends!

Follow the Patriots at www.loripiotrowski.com and sign up for my newsletter for information about speaking engagements, book signings, fun facts I find while researching, and upcoming releases!

ADDENDA

COMMISSIONERS OF CUSTOMS ACT - JUNE 29, 1767

An Act to Enable His Majesty to Put the Customs, and Other Duties, in the British Dominions in America, and the Execution of the Laws Relating to Trade There, under the Management of Commissioners to be Appointed for that Purpose, and to be Resident in the Said Dominions

WHEREAS in pursuance of an act of Parliament made in the twenty-fifth year of the reign of King Charles the Second, entitled, An act for the encouragement of the Greenland and Eastland trades, and for the better securing the plantation trade, the rates and duties imposed by that, and several subsequent acts of Parliament upon various goods imported into, or exported from the British colonies and plantations in America, have been put under the management of the commissioners of the customs in England for the time being, by and under the authority and directions of the high treasurer, or commissioners of the treasury for the time being; and whereas the officers appointed for the collection of the said rates and duties in America are obliged to apply to the said commissioners of the customs in England for their special instructions and directions, upon every particular doubt and difficulty which arises in relation to the payment of the said rates and duties, whereby all persons concerned in the commerce and trade of the said colonies and plantations are greatly obstructed and delayed in the carrying on and transacting of their business; and whereas the appointing of commissioners to be resident in some convenient part of his Majesty's dominions in America, and to be invested with such powers as are now exercised by the commissioners of the customs in England by virtue of the laws in being, would relieve the said merchants and traders from the said inconveniences, tend to the encouragement of commerce and to the better securing of the said rates and duties, by the more speedy and effectual collection thereof; be it therefore enacted by the King's most excellent Majesty, by and with the advice and consent of the Lords Spiritual and Temporal and Commons in this present Parliament assembled and by the authority of the same, that the customs and other duties imposed by any act or acts of Parliament upon any goods or merchandises brought or imported into, or exported or carried from any British colony or plantation in America, may from time to time be put under the management and direction of such commissioners to reside in the said plantations, as his Majesty, his heirs, and successors, by his or their commission or commissions under the great seal of Great Britain, shall judge to be most for the advantage of trade and security of the revenue of the said British colonies; any law, custom, or usage to the contrary notwithstanding.

II. And it is hereby further enacted by the authority aforesaid that the said commissioners to be appointed, or any three or more of them, shall have the same powers and authorities for carrying into execution the several laws relating to the revenues and trade of the said British colonies in America, as were, before the passing of this act, exercised by the commissioners of the customs in England, by virtue of any act or acts of Parliament now in force, and it shall and may be lawful to and for his Majesty, his heirs, and successors, in such commission or commissions, to make provision for putting in execution the several laws relating to the customs and trade of the said British colonies; any law, custom, or usage to the contrary notwithstanding.

III. Provided always, and it is hereby further enacted by the authority aforesaid, that all deputations and other authorities granted by the commissioners of the customs in England before the passing of this act, or which may be granted by them before any commission or commissions shall issue in pursuance of this act, to any officer or officers acting in the said colonies or plantations shall continue in force as fully, to all intents and purposes, as if this act had not been made, until the deputation, or other authorities so granted to such officer or officers, respectively, shall be revoked, annulled, or made void by the high treasurer of Great Britain, or commissioners of the treasury for the time being.

End Notes

1 *Boston Gazette, and Country Journal*, February 7, 1768.

2 *Boston Gazette, and Country Journal*, March 21, 1768.

3 Griffitts, Hannah. (1768). In *The Female Patriots. From Dissent in America*. R. F. Young, Ed. New York: Pearson Longman, 2005.

4 *Boston Gazette, and Country Living Journal*, August 8, 1768.

5 *Peter Oliver's Origin & Progress of the American Rebellion: A Tory View*. Douglass Adair and John A. Schutz, Eds. San Marino, CA: The Huntington Library, 1961. E263.M4040.

6 Nash, G. B. *The Unknown American Revolution: The Unruly Birth of Democracy and the Struggle to Create America*. New York: NY: Viking Penguin, 2005.

7 *Boston Gazette, and Country Journal*, October 2, 1769.

8 *Boston Gazette, and Country Journal*, October 30, 1769.

9 *Boston Gazette, and Country Journal*, February 26, 1770.

10 Wheatley, Phillis. "On The Death of Mr. Snider Murder'd By Richardson." (1768). AllPoetry.com. Accessed January 1, 2026. https://allpoetry.com/On-The-Death-of-Mr.-Snider-Murder'd-By-Richardson.

11 *Boston Gazette, and Country Living Journal*, February 26, 1770.

12 *Boston Gazette, and Country Living Journal*, March 5, 1770.

13 *Boston Gazette, and Country Journal*. March 5, 1770.

14 *Boston Gazette, and Country Living Journal*, March 5, 1770.

15 *Legal Papers of John Adams*, volume 2. From Adams Papers Digital Edition © 2020 Massachusetts Historical Society. http://www.masshist.org/publications/adams-papers/index.php/view/LJA03dg2.

References

Boston-Gazette, and Country Journal. (1765–1770.) Available on microfiche and at the Massachusetts Historical Society. The Annotated Newspapers of Harbottle Dorr. https://www.masshist.org/dorr/browse.

Brandow, James C. and William Senhouse. "Memoirs of a British Naval Officer at Boston, 1768-1769: Extracts from the Autobiography of William Senhouse." Proceedings of the Massachusetts Historical Society, Third Series, Vol. 105 (1993), pp. 74-93. Massachusetts Historical Society. https://www.jstor.org/stable/25081068. Accessed: 16-04-2019.

Carp. B. L. Rebels rising: Cities and the American Revolution. New York, NY: Oxford University Press, 2017.

Commissioners of Customs Act downloaded from Revolutionary War and Beyond. http://www.revolutionary-war-and-beyond.com/commissioners-of-customs-act-text.html.

Peter Oliver's Origin & Progress of the American Rebellion: A Tory View. 1961. Ed. by Douglass Adair and John A. Schutz. San Marino, CA: The Huntington Library. E263.M4040.

WEBSITE BIBLIOGRAPHY

The American Revenue Act of 1764 (the Sugar Act). http://www.americanhistorycentral.com/entry.php?rec=494

Artillery. http://www.AmericanRevolution.org/artillery.php

Boston 1775 http://www.boston1775.blogspot.com/

Encyclopedia Britannica. (2019). https://www.britannica.com/biography/James-Wolfe

The Quartering Act of 1765. http://www.ushistory.org/declaration/related/quartering.htm

Russell, Judy G. The True Gentleman. (2013) The Legal Genealogist. https://www.legalgenealogist.com/2013/04/22/the-true-gentleman/.

The Stamp Act. http://www.stamp-act-history.com. Text of the Stamp Act may be found at http://www.stamp-act-history.com/stamp-act/stamp-act-of-1765-original-text/

The Sugar Act of 1764. http://www.americanhistorycentral.com/entry.php?rec=494

The Sugar and Molasses Act of 1733. http://www.stamp-act-history.com/molasses-act/sugar-and-molasses-act-of-1733-original-text

MAP OF BOSTON

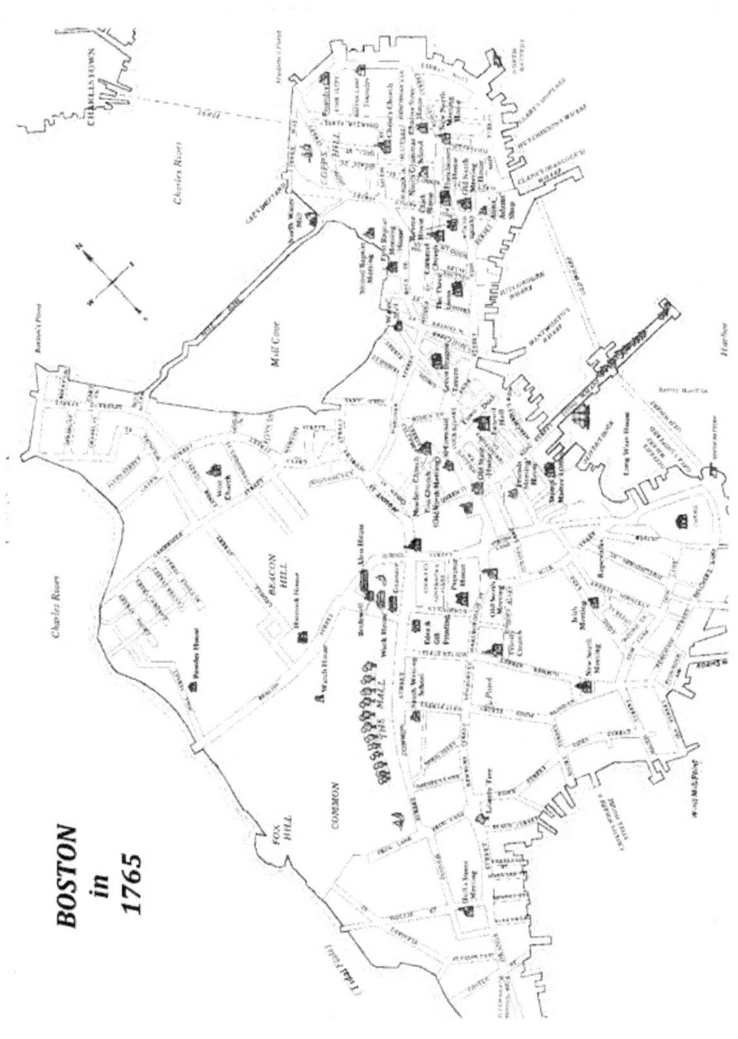

ACKNOWLEDGMENTS

A nod of appreciation to the Library of Congress librarians who, when I first started this project, let me know that newspapers of the era were on microfiche at the University of Nevada, Las Vegas, only a few miles from my home. Although I would have loved to travel to Washington and peruse these documents in the Reading Room, they did save me time and money! Special thanks to the Igniting Souls team, who supported my efforts to complete this trilogy. You are a valuable resource for authors around the world. Thank you.

ABOUT THE AUTHOR

Lori Piotrowski holds a master's degree in Romance Languages from The Ohio State University. She is a Renaissance woman of varied careers, including teaching Spanish and Portuguese for more than twenty years to college-aged students. Her career spans publishing, corporate communications, architectural photography, and public relations.

As a young girl, Lori's interest in reading was encouraged by her parents, who would turn off the TV and read every night. She watched their library grow and began her own private library by saving her allowance

Sydney Oster Photography

to buy books through the Scholastic Reader program at school. In college, she joined the Book of the Month club to create a more adult library. The first book she bought was Julia Child's *Mastering the Art of French Cooking*, which she still uses regularly. Her favorite day of the week is Friday, when she can leave all cares behind and curl up in an easy chair with a good read and one of her rescued felines.